CRITICAL ACCLAIM FOR ROBERT B. PARKER

'Parker writes old-time, stripped-to-the-bone, hard-boiled school of Chandler… His novels are funny, smart and highly entertaining… There's no writer I'd rather take on an aeroplane' – *Sunday Telegraph*

'Parker packs more meaning into a whispered "yeah" than most writers can pack into a page' – *Sunday Times*

'Why Robert Parker's not better known in Britain is a mystery. His best series featuring Boston-based PI Spenser is a triumph of style and substance' – *Daily Mirror*

'Robert B. Parker is one of the greats of the American hard-boiled genre' – *Guardian*

'Nobody does it better than Parker…' – *Sunday Times*

'Parker's sentences flow with as much wit, grace and assurance as ever, and Stone is a complex and consistently interesting new protagonist' – *Newsday*

'If Robert B. Parker doesn't blow it, in the new series he set up in Night Passage and continues with Trouble in Paradise, he could go places and take the kind of risks that wouldn't be seemly in his popular Spenser stories' – *New York Times*

ALSO BY ROBERT B. PARKER

THE SPENSER NOVELS

THE JESSE STONE MYSTERIES

Split Image
Fool Me Twice (by Michael Brandman)
Killing the Blues (by Michael Brandman)
Damned If You Do (by Michael Brandman)*
Blind Spot (by Reed Farrel Coleman)*
The Devil Wins (by Reed Farrel Coleman)*
Debt to Pay (by Reed Farrel Coleman)*
The Hangman's Sonnet (by Reed Farrel Coleman)*
Colorblind (by Reed Farrel Coleman)*
The Bitterest Pill (by Reed Farrel Coleman)*
Fool's Paradise (by Mike Lupica)*

THE SUNNY RANDALL MYSTERIES

Family Honor*
Perish Twice*
Shrink Rap*
Melancholy Baby*
Blue Screen*
Spare Change*
Blood Feud (by Mike Lupica)*
Grudge Match (by Mike Lupica)*
Payback (by Mike Lupica)*

ALSO BY ROBERT B. PARKER

Training with Weights (with John R. Marsh)
Three Weeks in Spring (with Joan Parker)
Wilderness
Love and Glory
Poodle Springs (with Raymond Chandler)
Perchance to Dream
A Year at the Races (with Joan Parker)
All Our Yesterdays
Gunman's Rhapsody
Double Play*
Appaloosa
Resolution
Brimstone
Blue Eyed Devil
Ironhorse (by Robert Knott)
Bull River (by Robert Knott)
The Bridge (by Robert Knott)
Blackjack (by Robert Knott)
Revelation (by Robert Knott)

*Available from No Exit Press

ROBERT B. PARKER'S
STONE'S THROW

A JESSE STONE MYSTERY

BY **MIKE LUPICA**

NO EXIT PRESS

First published in the UK in 2022 by No Exit Press,
an imprint of Oldcastle Books Ltd,
Harpenden, UK

noexit.co.uk
@noexitpress

A CIP catalogue record for this book is available from the British Library.

This is a work of fiction. Names, characters, places, and incidents either are
the product of the author's imagination or are used fictitiously, and any
resemblance to actual persons, living or dead, businesses, companies, events
or locales is entirely coincidental.

ISBN
978-0-85730-497-1 (print)
978-0-85730-498-8 (epub)

2 4 6 8 10 9 7 5 3 1

Typeset in 11.5 on 13.85pt Minion Pro
by Avocet Typeset, Bideford, Devon EX39 2BP
Printed and bound in Great Britain by CPI Group (UK) Ltd, Croydon, CR0 4YY

For more information about Crime Fiction go to @crimetimeuk

This book is for my editor,
and my friend, Sara Minnich.

ROBERT B. PARKER'S

STONE'S THROW

A JESSE STONE MYSTERY

1

Sunny Randall, with whom Jesse Stone was currently in a relationship time-out, asked him once what he missed the most about baseball. 'Everything,' he said.

'Even though it broke your heart?'

'Even though,' he said.

They'd been walking on the beach in Paradise, a couple miles from where he lived.

'Do you ever miss drinking the way you miss baseball?' Sunny said.

'Let me answer you this way,' Jesse said. 'The worst days I ever had because of drinking were the worst days I *ever* had. The worst day I ever had in baseball, at least until the one when I got hurt, was great.'

That day had been in Albuquerque, Triple-A ball, last stop before the majors, when he'd landed on his shoulder and had his dreams of making the show blow up along with his shoulder.

'What about sex?' Sunny asked.

Jesse had grinned.

'Right here?' Jesse said. 'Damn it, I *knew* I should have brought a blanket.'

'You know what I mean,' she said. 'Baseball or sex?'

'Sex with you, or sex in general?'

'In general.'

'Baseball,' he said.

'Seriously?'

'Both pleasurable activities, more with you than anyone I've ever known,' he said. 'But baseball wasn't just what I did. Was who I was.'

'I thought being a cop was who you are.'

'Now it is,' he said.

It was one of the last times they'd been together before she went to Los Angeles on a case a few weeks later, unsure of when she would return. She'd been hired by an old boyfriend of hers named Tony Gault, a big-time talent agent Out There whom she still refused to classify as having been her boyfriend, describing him more accurately, she said, as an itch she'd occasionally felt the urge to scratch. Jesse had met Gault, who wasn't much different from a lot of Hollywood phonies he'd met when he was still working Robbery Homicide for the LAPD. He'd told Sunny, and more than once, that the next time she had a similar itch she should consider ointment.

But they both knew they hadn't taken this time-out because of the case, or because she was there right now and he was here. They'd decided to take a break because they both knew they needed one. They loved each other, Jesse was certain of that. But she still loved her ex-husband, who had recently helped save her life from some very bad Russians on a case she'd been working. In the aftermath of that, she told Jesse that despite her best intentions, she was still feeling an old, almost gravitational pull in her ex's direction, no matter how hard she fought it.

'I don't pull,' he told her.

'Or push.'

'Nor that.'

'Why I love you,' Sunny said.

'Just not enough?'

'I didn't say that,' she said.

'Didn't have to,' Jesse said.

'Let me ask another question about baseball,' Sunny had said that night.

'As a way of changing the subject?'

'As a way of circling back to the original.'

'Do I need a lawyer before answering?'

'You hate lawyers,' Sunny had said.

'Well,' Jesse said. 'There's that.'

'Are you as *happy* with me as you were playing baseball?'

'Right now,' he said, 'or in general?'

'In general,' she said. 'And I don't need to remind the witness that he's still under oath.'

When Jesse took too long to answer she'd said, 'A full stop like that could hurt a girl's feelings.'

'You didn't even let me answer.'

'Didn't have to,' Sunny had said.

He had been thinking a lot about baseball the past few days, even more than usual, because he had to decide whether or not to play in the Paradise Men's Softball League, about to start up in a few weeks. The men's league, the kind of bar league he used to play in when he was in L.A., wasn't like real baseball, Jesse knew that. Or even close. But close enough. And all the ball he had now. He couldn't make the kind of throw from shortstop that he used to be able to make when he still had the arm. Sometimes in the morning, when he was sitting on the side of the bed, he would rotate his right shoulder and hear what sounded like loose coins rattling around in a clothes dryer.

But he could still make that throw better than even young studs in the league just out of college. Jesse smiled now, to himself, as he walked the same beach he'd walked with Sunny, just walked it in the night, with her Out There and him here. Knowing that's the way all old guys thought, all the old ballplayers who were sure they would have made the show if things had broken differently for them.

But I would have made it.

He was on another one of his late-night long walks. He had been taking a lot of them lately, more since Sunny had left. He was still running a few miles a day, a few days a week. But it was getting harder for him to do that, because his knees had begun to bark at him the way his shoulder did. More old-man shit that he knew wasn't going to get any better, or easier, the older he got. Whoever had said it in Hollywood had been right. Getting old wasn't for sissies.

Especially when they were old ballplayers.

These were the things you thought about out here, the things you couldn't stop yourself from remembering, sometimes coming at you like the waves.

But it was better for him to be in motion than sitting at home, the time of night in his drinking days when he'd fall asleep in front of the television, in his chair or on the floor, passed out after trying to watch a Red Sox game. Ballgames on television still made him think about drinking. But, then, what the hell didn't? Even thinking about softball made him think about drinking, that first cold one when the game was over that Suitcase Simpson always described as 'the best beer of the week.'

So he walked, sometimes through the streets of Paradise, sometimes along the water. Tonight he had decided on the water, Jesse making it all the way down to the piece of land, high up above him to his right, that had been pulling the town apart, the one nicknamed The Throw.

It was the last and biggest and absolutely most valuable piece of oceanfront property in Paradise, Mass, having been put up for sale by the rich asshat Thomas Lawton III, who owned it, now being fought over by two even richer men who wanted to buy it from him and develop the shit out of it. And because it was their stated plan to develop it, the sale had to be approved by the Board of Selectmen.

One bidder was Billy Singer, Vegas guy. The other was Ed Barrone, a Boston developer who'd recently built two of the first non-tribal casinos in Massachusetts. Both had made no secret of the fact that they wanted to build a hotel and casino at The Throw. Both had been hard-lobbying the Board of Selectmen to approve the sale of the land, before each submitted his final bid. Both had spent an insane amount of money advertising in local media, promising jobs that both men swore would finally bring the town's economy back from the damage COVID-19 had done. Doing what guys like them always did, no matter the prize:

Showing they'd be willing to fight to the death over dirt.

Jesse made his way up there now, first through the dunes, then the long path that led up to the eastern end of the property, which had one of the great views of the ocean in Massachusetts, or anywhere else.

It was where they'd found the first shallow grave about a month ago, with this miniature headstone, made of lightweight concrete, next to it:

R.I.P. PARADISE

The headstone had the date the town had officially been incorporated in the nineteenth century, and this year's date. The responsibility for the graves – or credit – had been accepted freely by the local group, mostly kids, known as the 'SOB.' Completely without irony. Or maybe just a little bit. Save Our Beach. They really saw themselves as saving Paradise and its ecosystem from these two grubby developers, no matter how many jobs Singer and Barrone were promising. The owner of The Throw, Lawton, the last living member of the Lawton family, had another name for them. He had taken to derisively calling them 'the tree huggers,' and constantly hectoring Jesse to find every one of them vandalizing his property and throw their asses in jail.

'For digging holes?' Jesse'd said to him the last time he'd come barging into Jesse's office. 'You mean before the bulldozers come rolling through your property like the First Army?'

All in all, Jesse thought, he needed an old-fashioned land grab like this the way he needed to fall off the goddamn wagon. Jesse knew that Singer had hated Barrone from the time Ed Barrone had tried to invade his turf in Vegas. The feud between the two men only got worse when Barrone got the casinos in Taunton and Springfield that Singer wanted. Barrone hated Singer for being a mobbed-up Vegas guy thinking he could come east and throw his weight and money around as a way of getting even with him. They were both the real SOBs in the story, to Jesse's way of thinking. The only thing on which Singer and Barrone agreed was that each man hated the tree huggers as much as Thomas Lawton did, because the kids weren't just digging graves, they were attacking all of them on social media on a daily basis, vowing to continue their fight even if the Board of Selectmen had voted to approve the sale, which everybody in Paradise assumed it would in the end; there was simply too much money at stake, too many jobs. By now the whole thing had turned the whole town meaner than the place Jesse called Tweeterville. Choosing sides on the sale of the land. Choosing sides on the men bidding to buy it.

The Throw felt serene to Jesse in the night, almost like sacred ground, with the sound of the ocean behind Jesse now and the cloudless sky full of stars. In this moment it was impossible for him to believe that a piece of earth as beautiful and previously undeveloped had turned, at least symbolically, into a war zone.

Jesse had his flashlight out, and now spotted what looked to be a new grave up ahead, just without a headstone next to it this time.

Shit, he thought.

Not because the tree huggers had come back. Just because a new grave meant more work for him, because their latest effort would mean another visit from young Thomas Lawton in the morning, and a continuation of his bitch-a-thon.

Only this grave, Jesse saw when he stared down into it, was different.

This one had a body inside it.

His boss's.

2

'The mayor shot himself in the middle of The Throw?' Suitcase Simpson said when he got there.

'To be determined,' Jesse said.

Neil O'Hara. Not just Jesse's boss. His friend. One who'd ended up in the middle of the war between Singer and Barrone and the middle of the campaign about the sale. One who'd been fighting the deal in vain, trying to convince his constituents that there were more important things than money.

'And I'd finally started thinking of him as the mayor,' Suit said.

For as long as anybody could remember, the true mayor of Paradise had been the president of the Board of Selectmen. They had finally decided the year before to make it an elective office. Neil had then won the town's first-ever mayoral race, Gary Armistead running as his deputy. They had won by a lot. People liked Neil O'Hara.

Just not everybody.

Jesse said, 'Doesn't do him much good now.'

By now, Jesse had done everything by the numbers. Called 911. Called Ellis Munroe, Paradise's new district attorney and no friend to the Paradise Police Department, who'd called Brian Lundquist at the state police, who'd sent two of his guys over. For once, Jesse and Munroe had managed to get through a conversation without arguing. He had made no secret, from the time he'd gotten the job, that he was the most powerful law enforcement figure in the town, and in the county. Not Jesse. And had made it clear to Jesse that it was a new day in law enforcement in America, maybe he'd noticed, it had been in all the papers, and that the days when prosecutors let cops make up the rules as they went along were long gone.

'I know you don't need my guys,' Lundquist had said on the phone. 'But my boss got the ass last time we didn't have our people there first thing.'

It had been when Lily Cain had shot herself, on the other side of town. A member of one of Paradise's royal families, the way Thomas Lawton was.

'We've all got bosses,' Jesse said.

'You don't,' Lundquist said.

Jesse had called Dev Chadha, the medical examiner. Called Molly Crane, knowing there would be holy hell to pay later in the morning if he didn't, and Suit, and Gabe Weathers. They all knew how crucial the first two hours were, that missed evidence – whether it was a suicide or a homicide – could be devastating to an investigation later on. Suit liked to tell Jesse that he didn't just do things by the book, he acted sometimes like he'd written the book.

It was past two in the morning now, a couple hours after Jesse had discovered the body and the SIG P365, the expensive XL model, next to Neil's right hand in the dirt.

R.I.P., Jesse thought.

The body of Neil O'Hara had finally been bagged and loaded into the van and taken to Dev's lab. Jesse had once again reminded Suit and Molly that only amateurs wanted a body transported away from the scene as quickly as possible.

'Can I do the rest of it?' Molly Crane said, grinning at him. 'By now, pretty sure I know it by heart.'

'Knock yourself out,' Jesse said.

'You want your ME's eyes on the scene as long as possible,' Molly said.

Suit picked it up from there.

'Can't have too many sets of eyes,' Suit said.

'Am I really that entertaining to the two of you?' Jesse said.

'Endlessly,' Molly said.

They had been through this enough times by now, Jesse and Molly and Suit, to know that they weren't disrespecting the victim, or his memory, with humor or snark. They weren't trying to normalize what had happened, whatever had happened, and how Neil O'Hara, a good guy, had ended up here. But Neil wasn't Jesse's friend now, or mayor. Or husband of Kate. He was their vic. He was whatever case number Molly would give him when they were at the station later, and what was going to be a shitshow began almost immediately.

Molly said, 'Why would Neil kill himself?'

'If he killed himself,' Jesse said.

'Sorry,' she said. '*If*.'

'You want the whole list, or just a partial?' Jesse said. 'Problems at home. He got caught embezzling money. He found out he was sick. He found out Kate was sick. Or she'd been cheating on him. He found out her secrets, or had some of his own. Or just one big one. Maybe it was just depression.'

They'd stepped away from the grave.

'Twenty-five million people in this country suffer from depression every year,' he said. Almost talking to himself now. 'Half of the people who kill themselves suffer from major depression. If you include alcoholics who are goddamn depressed, it goes from fifty percent to seventy-five.'

He stopped and smiled at both of them.

'You learn a lot about depression in rehab,' he said. 'Their position is that safe is a hell of a lot better than sorry.'

'He's the chief,' Suit said to Molly. 'He even knows shit he *didn't* learn in rehab.'

Gabe had taken foot castings from the grass around the grave. Dev had cut Neil O'Hara's fingernails before he left, and checked them, and his hands, for gunpowder residue. Jesse had been the one to bag the SIG, and handed it over to Lundquist's detectives, Crandall and Scoppetta, both solid cops with whom he had worked before.

Jesse walked away from Molly and Suit, wanting to think, wanting to absorb the scene, making a long, slow circle, walking toward the ocean and then back around, toward the

17

woods. The Throw. Not prime real estate now. This was a crime scene, involving a man who, even before he became mayor, when he was just a member of the Board, had saved Jesse's job more than once when Jesse was still a drunk.

With all that, Jesse couldn't help himself, he felt the way he did when he was a kid before the first pitch of a game, a combination of excitement and adrenaline and even fear. If it was suicide, he would find out why. If it was murder, made to look like suicide, he would find out who did that to Neil O'Hara, because he owed him that.

He didn't need Dix, his therapist, to explain why something as bad as this made the cop in him feel this good. Dix knew. He'd been a cop himself. A cop *was* who Jesse was now. Sometimes all he was.

Peter Perkins came walking over to them, from the west side of the property. He'd been over to Neil's house, said his car was in the garage.

'You go through the house?' Jesse said.

'I was waiting for you to give me the go-ahead.'

'Go ahead,' Jesse said.

Jesse told Molly and Suit to make another sweep of the property, and then another one after that. Jesse told them he was going to drive over to Neil's old house, the one on Stiles Island in which he'd lived before he and his wife separated, and break the news to his wife.

'Estranged wife,' Molly said.

'Still his wife,' Jesse said.

'You sure you want to be the one?' Molly said.

Jesse knew what she meant. Jesse had been involved with Kate O'Hara once, the last relationship she'd had before she'd married Neil. It hadn't lasted long, but had been fairly intense while it did. He was still drinking then. Sometimes he wondered if it was as intense as he remembered, or if it just felt that way because he *was* still a drunk.

'It should be me,' Jesse said. 'He was my friend. She's still my friend, even though I haven't seen much of her lately.'

He noticed Molly staring past him then, out toward the woods in the distance, her eyes suddenly wide, her focus nearly fervid, everything about her completely alert. He had seen this look from her plenty of times before, the full force of her directed at someone, or something.

'What's wrong?' Jesse said.

'Thought I saw a ghost,' Molly Crane said.

3

Sometimes Jesse thought he would rather find a dead body, bullet through the eye, than talk to the survivors, especially when they were survivors he knew.

Not only knew.

But with whom he had history.

He assumed by now, because Paradise was such a small town, that the only people who didn't know he had history with Kate Alexander O'Hara were either dead or in Europe.

Jesse and Kate had broken off their relationship long before she started seeing Neil. After that, Neil and Kate had gotten very serious, very quickly. Both of them had been married before. Jesse knew how much Kate wanted to be married again. Six months after she and Neil had started dating, they were holding a Paradise wedding, with all the trimmings, in that Episcopal church on Main Street. Then he heard they separated about six months ago. She was still living in the house on Stiles Island, in a small gated community called The Bluffs, even though there weren't any bluffs within a couple miles. Neil had moved to a house in town.

Jesse had been to the Stiles Island house for dinner after Neil had been elected, and drove there now, over the Stiles Island Bridge, not needing Waze, remembering where Neil and Kate had lived when they were together. He had considered waiting until the sun was up, but then couldn't think of one good reason why that would make what he had to do any easier. This was the modern world of social media, after all. No matter how much you tried to button up news like this, it would get out. Why? Because it always did, because trying to stop Twitter and Facebook and Instagram and all the rest of it was like trying to stop a speeding train.

The information highway, Jesse thought. *What a joy.*

As he got out of the car, he wished now he had brought Molly with him.

There were no lights from inside the house, but why would there be at this time of night? Jesse took in a lot of air, felt as if he let out even more, headed up the walk.

As he did, there was a splash of light in front of the house, and Kate O'Hara had opened the front door.

'I was afraid I might startle you,' he said.

'You live alone,' she said, 'you go with a doorbell cam these days.'

Then she said, 'Something's happened to Neil, hasn't it?'

She was as beautiful as ever, even with her senses clearly on high alert now, even having just been awakened, hair shorter than it was the last time he'd seen her, wearing sweatpants and a T-shirt that read NOT ARGUING. EXPLAINING.

'Let's go inside,' Jesse said.

'Was he in some kind of accident?' she said.

'Not out here,' Jesse said.

'You can tell me out here as well as you can tell me inside,' she said. 'Goddamn it, Jesse, what happened?'

He stood there on the front porch and told her what he'd found. It was as if all the air came out of her once he did, and she started to slide down the doorframe. He caught her before she fell and walked her inside and sat her down on the couch in the living room and turned on the antique light at one end of it. She curled into a corner of the couch and hugged herself, gently rocking from side to side. Jesse sat at the other end of the couch. Everyone reacted differently, with both shock and grief. Some cried, some got hysterical. Some people collapsed within themselves the way Kate had. Some showed no reaction at all.

'Tell me what you found,' she said.

He told her what he'd discovered in the shallow grave. The gun next to him. He asked when the last time she'd seen him was. She said three or four days ago, she couldn't remember exactly which one, he was stopping around all the time, always talking about wanting them to try again. She was rambling. Jesse let her go.

Just like that, she stopped herself.

'Neil killed himself?' she said. 'Is that what you're telling me?'

'I'm telling you that he might have,' he said. 'But that doesn't mean he did. This all just happened.'

He thought of a case Sunny had worked on, one of the principals in it made to look like a suicide victim. But it wasn't one. And it didn't matter.

'Say it was,' Jesse said. 'Could you possibly have seen it?'

She waited before answering.

'Could I *possibly* have seen it?' she said. 'You mean if I'd tried a little harder or cared a little more?'

'I didn't mean it that way,' Jesse said.

'He'd been under a lot of pressure because of the land deal, but he was always under some kind of pressure,' she said. 'Maybe he was showing signs of depression and I just missed them. But then he'd always done a good job of hiding that side of himself.'

'He was depressed about not being able to stop the deal from going through?'

'That, mostly,' Kate O'Hara said. 'But there was more. He kept thinking we were going to get back together, no matter how

21

many times I told him, as gently as I could, that wasn't going to happen. His world had gotten smaller. I wanted mine to expand, and not here. My honest opinion? I think events were just ganging up on him.' She rubbed her eyes, hard. 'Is it impossible for me to believe that he might have killed himself? It's not.'

She sighed.

'Neil was a pleaser, Jesse,' she said. 'But it didn't help him this time. The majority of the people in town wanted this sale. He felt he should have done more to persuade them they were wrong.'

'He told me one time that he thought he knew what it would be like to be mayor,' Jesse said. 'But he hadn't signed on to feel like a real estate agent closing a deal.'

'He was almost morally opposed to this deal,' she said. 'But he was a politician, too, which made him a pragmatist. It was another reason why this was eating him up inside.'

'Might there have been money problems in his life?'

She said, 'Not having to do with me.'

Jesse shook his head. 'Didn't mean that, either.'

'Sorry,' she said. 'I'm still trying to process this.'

'Lot to process,' Jesse said.

'Maybe he got tired of fighting,' she said. 'I feel guilty now that I couldn't get as obsessed about the deal as he was. But when we did get together, it was all he wanted to talk about. He even wanted to have dinner last night, as a matter-of-fact. I'll always regret turning him down.'

'No way you could have known.'

'I just didn't want to hear about The Throw all over again,' she said. 'Does that make me a bad person?'

Jesse was already thinking he should leave now, talk to her again later. They hadn't been alone together in a long time. But whatever they'd had, for as long as they'd had it, there was still something in the air they were breathing, and he wondered if she still felt it as well. Or maybe he had it all wrong. The older he got, the less he knew about women. Proof being Sunny. He'd thought what he and Sunny had was damn near perfect, until it wasn't.

Suddenly a single tear appeared on her cheek. She reached up absently and brushed it away.

'Neil...,' she said. She stopped, then started again. 'Neil is what this town is supposed to be, as quaint a notion as that is.'

'I know,' Jesse said, because he did know.

There was nothing more for now. Jesse stood. So did she. She covered the few feet between them and gently kissed him on the cheek. Everything was familiar again as soon as she did, the feel of her, the smell of her. He started to put his arms around her, almost by habit, but did not.

'It was nice of you to tell me in person,' she said.

'I felt I owed it to you.'

'You never owed me anything,' she said.

She walked him to the door.

'I owe *him*,' Jesse said.

'Somebody once said Neil was a friend behind your back,' Kate said.

He smiled at her now, and shrugged.

'I feel like there's something more I should say,' he said. 'But beats the hell out of me what it might be.'

'I couldn't live with him any longer,' she said. 'But I still loved him.'

Jesse gave her a long look.

'Do *you* think he killed himself?' Kate O'Hara said.

'Beats the hell out of me,' Jesse said again.

4

Molly sat across from Jesse, their usual window table at Daisy Dyke's diner, just after seven in the morning, neither one of them having slept. They were meeting the new mayor, Gary Armistead, at the station in an hour.

Overture to the shitshow, Jesse thought.

Daisy was waiting on them. She already knew what had happened to Neil O'Hara, whom she said had eaten breakfast here almost every morning, including yesterday. Jesse asked what they had talked about. Daisy said Neil had wanted to know if she might be the last person in the state of Massachusetts calling herself a dyke. Daisy had informed him there were still Dyke Marches in various locations across the country every June.

'He told me he'd pay if I had one down Main Street,' Daisy said. She shook her head.

'Goddamn, this is a kick in the nuts,' Daisy said.

Her hair was streaked with blue this spring. When Molly remarked on it, Daisy said she'd seen an old picture of Lady Gaga with blue hair and decided to go for it, what the hell, you were only gay once.

She poured both of them more coffee.

'How's Sunny?' she said to Jesse now.

'In L.A.,' he said. 'But we'd decided to take a time-out before she left.'

'You think I didn't already know that, putz?' she said.

When she walked away, Molly said, 'Did you ask Kate if Neil owned a gun?'

'Right before I pulled away,' Jesse said. 'She said he hated guns. But that doesn't mean he couldn't have put his hands on one. She said anybody could these days.'

'The staties already ran the one we found,' she said. 'Not even a 4473.'

Proof of ownership.

'So it came from where most guns come from,' Jesse said.

'Somewhere,' Molly said.

Jesse drank coffee. 'I can't see him doing this,' he said.

'I knew him practically my whole life,' Molly said. 'Neither can I.'

Jesse stared out the window.

'Something's bothering you,' she said.

'A lot is bothering me,' he said.

'Personal or professional?' she said.

'Professional,' he said.

'That means you don't want to talk about Sunny,' Molly said.

'Daisy took care of that.'

'So she did,' Molly said. 'Putz.'

'Seems to be the consensus,' he said.

'So what's the professional?' she said.

'Where were the footprints?' he said. 'That's one thing. Other than mine, there were no footprints around that grave.'

'It had rained earlier in the evening,' Molly said. 'Maybe he did it before it rained.'

'Or somebody just dumped him there and then brought something with him to cover his tracks, from the end of the dirt road and back,' Jesse said. 'Especially back, if he'd carried the body to the grave.'

'Lot of work,' Molly said.

'Not to make it look like he killed himself when he didn't,' Jesse said.

'Anything else?' she said.

'It's probably nothing,' Jesse said. 'But Dev said the bullet ended up behind Neil's right eye. But the gun was in the dirt above his head. Almost like somebody had just tossed it into the grave.'

'Teach me, *sensei*,' she said.

'Somebody who shoots themself has no control over where the gun ends up, they usually die instantly,' Jesse said. 'But Dev says the bullet was behind his right eye. I had a case once in L.A. We had to keep testing the gun to see if it could have landed in the position it did next to the body. And no matter how many times we tested it, we finally decided it couldn't have ended up where it did.'

'You're gonna do that, aren't you?'

'Eventually.'

'How long ago was that case in L.A.?' Molly said. 'Just out of curiosity.'

'Long,' Jesse said.

She grinned. 'You know what drinking didn't do with you? Kill brain cells.'

'So far, so good.'

'Probably no point in stressing on it until you get Dev's full report,' she said.

'I've been stressing since I looked down into that grave and saw who it was,' Jesse said.

Now Molly was the one staring out the window, chin in hand. She never seemed to age. Jesse just assumed that Molly Crane would still have her looks, and her marbles, when she was eighty.

'You worried about Michael?' Jesse said.

Her husband. Last year he had crewed for a hedge-funder named Teddy Altman in the Trans Pacific race. Now he was with Altman in a new race across the Atlantic.

'Michael Crane against the ocean?' she said. 'My money would be on my cutie.'

'You've got that look,' Jesse said. He grinned. 'The one where you're almost having a deep thought.'

'Very funny,' she said.

She had been working up to something. But Jesse knew her well enough to know she'd get there when she was ready.

Finally she turned back to him and said, 'Remember at The Throw when I said I thought I saw a ghost? Well, it wasn't just a figure of speech.'

Jesse waited.

'I thought I saw Crow,' she said.

5

'Your Native American friend,' Jesse said.

'Good for you for not saying "Indian,"' Molly said.

'Even the Cleveland Indians aren't going to be the Indians for much longer. And the Redskins aren't the Red-skins.'

'And don't call him my friend,' Molly said.

'He did have benefits, though.'

They had first met Wilson Cromartie, who claimed he was Apache, when he was part of a crew, Jimmy Macklin's, that had blown up the Stiles Island Bridge and essentially taken everybody who lived over there hostage. Jesse had lost two of his cops during the siege. Finally had gotten to Stiles by boat and shot Macklin dead. Molly had been the one to capture Macklin's girlfriend. When it was all over, Cromartie – known as Crow – had gotten away with millions of dollars, actual amount still unknown to Jesse.

Crow had gotten away on a speedboat. Jesse was sure that it was the last he would ever see of him. But he came back to Paradise ten years later, outside the statute of limitations for the money with which he'd gotten away, denying that he had killed anybody before he took off up the coast. At the time he was tracking down the runaway daughter of a Florida gangster. But then Crow decided he couldn't give the girl, Amber Francisco, back to a bum like her father. Jesse helped him save the kid from the father's men. The father later ended up dead. With no way of knowing or ever proving it, Jesse assumed that Crow had just gone down to South Florida and gotten it done, before disappearing again.

While Crow had been in Paradise the second time, he had spent one night with Molly Crane, the first and only infidelity in her marriage to Michael, another time when Michael had been out of town. Other than Molly and Crow, only Jesse knew what had happened between them. Michael Crane, according to Molly, had never found out that the mother of their four children, a Catholic almost as Catholic as a bishop, had slept not just with another man, but a criminal.

Jesse had always thought he understood the need upon which Molly had acted that night. It was the same sort of need, bordering on obsession, that he'd had for Jenn, during their marriage and long after it had ended, no matter how much she slept around.

Crow had been like that for Molly Crane. There was no way to know what would have happened if he had stayed in Paradise, what further damage she might have done to her marriage, and to her career. But she never had to find out. He left after he and Jesse had saved Amber Francisco.

Now she thought he was back.

'We don't even know if he was really an Apache,' Molly said.

'One of many things we don't know about Crow.'

'He could have been lying about that.'

'Hard to believe,' Jesse said. 'A button man and thief being that unreliable. What can you even believe in anymore?'

'But you admitted you couldn't have saved Amber without him,' Molly said. 'In a way, you used him, too.'

Jesse grinned.

'Strange bedfellows,' he said. 'So to speak.'

'Sunny's right,' Molly said. 'You're not as funny as you think you are.'

'Why are we back to talking about Sunny?' Jesse said.

'Oh,' Molly said, 'so you can bust my chops about Crow and I can't bust yours about her?'

'You're the one who thinks she saw him,' Jesse said. 'If it was him.'

'And if it was,' Molly said, 'what was he doing there after we found Neil's body?'

28

Jesse waved at Daisy for the check. She smiled and gave him the finger and told him to get lost.

'I've put off going to the station as long as possible,' Jesse said.

'You get to hold a press conference,' Molly said, 'just like a big boy.'

'I could just barricade myself in my office,' Jesse said.

Molly smacked her forehead. 'Why didn't I think of that?'

They came around the corner and saw the television trucks parked on both sides of the street and the microphone set up just outside the front door, the media beginning to form what Jesse imagined to be a gaggle of geese.

Jesse stopped and sighed.

'Any last words, soldier?' Molly said.

'Fuckety fuck,' Jesse said.

'The first one's not even a real word,' Molly said.

6

Before Jesse walked back outside to face the media an hour later, Molly told him to make sure to put on his best face.

'I left it at home,' he said.

'You want me to run over and get it?' she said.

There were two more TV trucks by then, both from Boston stations. Jesse could no longer remember at which one Jenn had worked, first as a weather girl. She'd later moved up to news by sleeping with the station manager, Jesse thinking that likely wasn't a course taught at the best journalism schools.

The rest of the people in front of him, he assumed now, were print and radio reporters. Jesse understood why they were all here. An old friend from the *Los Angeles Times* had once told him that the two biggest stories were war and big guy dies. So it was today, even though the big guy was just the top politician in a small town.

Nellie Shofner, from the Paradise *Town Crier*, was in the front row. Jesse kept waiting for her to be hired away by the *Globe* or a bigger paper somewhere else. Or end up on television, since she had both the talent and the looks for that – even though if he ever said that out loud, the looks part, he would probably have been on his way to Weinstein Island.

For now, though, she was still in Paradise, practically a one-person staff on the *Crier*. Jesse liked her. Not as much, Molly and Suit were fond of saying, as she seemed to like him.

Jesse made a brief opening statement about finding Neil's body in the middle of the night, and then called on Nellie first.

'Chief Stone,' she said, 'is Mr O'Hara's death officially being classified as a suicide at this point?'

'It is being classified as an unattended death,' he said.

He saw Nellie grin.

'Would you care to elaborate?'

'No,' Jesse said.

'Does it mean you think it might not be a suicide?'

Jesse said, 'I think it is an unattended death.'

Jesse looked over at Gary Armistead and Ellis Munroe. They both shook their heads, as if Jesse were back to being a town drunk. Munroe, who Jesse knew had been a wrestler at Harvard, looked tougher. Armistead was definitely prettier.

Jesse called on Wayne Cosgrove then, Sunny's columnist friend from the *Globe*.

'Was it his own gun?' Cosgrove said.

'It was *a* gun,' Jesse said.

Now Cosgrove grinned.

'You always this forthcoming, Chief?' he said.

'On a good day,' Jesse said.

He answered a few more questions, none to the satisfaction of those asking them, before Armistead stepped to the microphone, ready for his first close-up as mayor.

'As always,' he said, 'Chief Stone is a man of few words.' He smiled. 'Occasionally they're even well chosen.'

Jesse whispered to Molly, 'I've got a few words for Gary, actually.'

She poked him hard with an elbow.

'I just want everybody to know that the chief and his people will get to the bottom of this tragedy,' Armistead said.

He paused and said, 'But having said that, even as Chief Stone begins his investigation, the town needs to get back to the important work of finalizing the sale of The Throw.'

Jesse whispered to Molly, 'Sure, the body must be good and cold by now.'

And got himself poked again.

By the time Armistead was answering his first question, Jesse was inside his office, sitting behind his desk, reaching into his bottom drawer and taking out his old glove and the ball he kept with it, snapping the ball into the pocket with a flick of his wrist, the sound of that as loud and sweet to him as ever.

He put the glove away and opened his laptop and saw the email from Scoppetta, telling him that the only gun residue they'd found had been on the right hand of Neil O'Hara.

The same Neil O'Hara who had been the left-handed throwing and left-handed hitting first baseman on Jesse's softball team, and the left-handed tennis player whom he'd occasionally see on one of Paradise's public courts.

He was considering the odds and probabilities of that, someone firing a gun to kill himself with his off hand, when Suit poked his head in.

'Somebody here to see you,' he said to Jesse.

'Friend or foe?' Jesse said.

'For you to know and me to find out,' Suit said.

He shut the door behind him and stepped into the office and lowered his voice and said, 'It's Crow.'

7

His long hair, so black it reminded Jesse of a blued gun barrel, but now sprinkled just slightly with gray, was tied into a ponytail. There were more lines around his eyes than Jesse remembered. Crow hadn't gotten any younger since they had teamed up to save Amber Francisco from her father. But then who had?

He was as lean as ever, all sinew and hard edges and quiet menace. *Especially that,* Jesse thought. *All* that. There would never be any way of knowing how many men Crow had killed in his life, or how much money he'd gotten away with when he'd been on Jimmy Macklin's crew and held Stiles Island for ransom.

But Jesse was sure it had been a lot, had always assumed it had been the score of a lifetime for Wilson Cromartie.

He wore black jeans, a black western shirt, buttoned to the neck, silver buttons. Crow settled into the chair across from Jesse, in which he had sat before.

Crow nodded at him.

'How come you don't have that top drawer to your right open?' he said. 'One with the gun in it.'

'I feel as if our relationship, such as it is, has evolved,' Jesse said.

'You're saying you trust me now?'

Hint of amusement in his dark eyes. Not much. As if they'd briefly been flecked with light.

'You know better,' Jesse said. Jerked his head in the direction of the Keurig machine to Crow's right. 'Coffee?'

'You got any of that matcha green tea?' Crow said. 'I've acquired a taste for it.'

Jesse said, 'This isn't Starbucks.'

'I take that as a no?'

'Yes.'

'Then I'm good,' Crow said.

He and Crow had never been bears for small talk, so Jesse wasn't now.

'You were at my crime scene last night,' he said.

'Who says?'

His voice still sounded like the raspy whisper that became more pronounced with Clint Eastwood the older he got.

'Molly saw you,' Jesse said.

'Paradise Police Department,' Crow said. 'Ever vigilant.'

'We try.'

'I didn't see Molly out there when I came in,' Crow said.

'Maybe she didn't want to be seen.'

'How's she doing?'

Jesse smiled. 'None of your business.'

Crow smiled. Jesse noticed a single gold tooth, upper right, that he didn't remember having been there before.

'I come in peace,' Crow said.

'You left out "paleface,"' Jesse said.

'My people have evolved, too.'

'You really Apache?'

'None of *your* business.'

'What were you doing at The Throw?'

'I was walking back to my house and saw the flashing lights.'

'At that time of night.'

'I'm nocturnal,' Crow said. 'Like you.'

'You have a house here?' Jesse said.

'Airbnb,' Crow said. 'Paradise side of the bridge.'

'A bridge you blew one time.'

'The others did that,' Crow said. 'Not me.'

'Accessory after the fact,' Jesse said.

'Allegedly.'

'The money you stole wasn't.'

Crow grinned. 'See previous answer.'

'What are you doing here?' Jesse said.

'Billy Singer's an old acquaintance of mine, guess you could say. He sent me to look out for his interests. He knew I had history here.'

'Do you ever.'

'He really wants that land.'

'I'm aware,' Jesse said.

They stared at each other.

'You happen to have an alibi for the hours before you say you saw all the flashing lights?'

'Do I need one?'

'Humor me.'

'Was with a lady,' he said.

'She have a name?'

'You want her married name?'

Jesse grinned. 'Old dog,' he said. 'Old tricks.'

'It was the dead guy's wife,' Crow said.

Didn't see that coming.

'You're telling me you were with Kate O'Hara last night,' Jesse said.

'Not the way you think. And not for very long.'

'Kind of a coincidence,' Jesse said, 'in light of what happened to her husband later that same night.'

'Only if you believe in that shit,' Crow said.

'So why were you with her?'

'Trying to gather as much information as possible, from all sides,' Crow said. 'Billy thinks information is power.'

'So did Bugsy Siegel,' Jesse said.

'Vegas is different now,' Crow said.

'Yeah,' Jesse said. 'More fountains.'

Jesse had done a lot of research on Billy Singer by now. And Ed Barrone. Singer had spent the last several years trying to bury the reputation for ruthlessness he'd acquired on the way up, mostly for burying people who'd gotten in his way.

'Put it this way,' another casino owner had said of Billy Singer in one of the stories Jesse had read. 'Billy goes into the corner, he's the one coming out with the puck.'

'What were you talking about with Kate?' Jesse said.

'I couldn't get ahold of her husband,' Crow said. 'And I wanted to get a sense of how much influence she might have with him.'

'Meet and greet,' Jesse said.

'You could put it that way.'

'But not trying to persuade her to persuade her husband.'

'Told you I've evolved.'

'My ass.'

'Ask you a question?' Crow said.

Jesse waited.

'If I was back here threatening people to get them on Billy's side of this, don't you think you would have heard about it?' Crow said.

'Unless you threatened them with what would happen to them if I did hear,' Jesse said. 'Another way of looking at it.'

'Least now I know why I couldn't track down O'Hara,' Crow said. 'Even though my people are noted trackers.' Crow shrugged. 'The closer the vote gets, Billy just wanted me to take some temperatures, see how many people were as conflicted as O'Hara.'

'So you'd met with Neil previously.'

'Couple days ago,' Crow said. 'Last night was supposed to be a follow-up.'

'How did he seem to you?'

'Like he knew the only thing left was finding out whether Billy or Barrone was going to be the last man standing on this thing.'

'You try to give him a little shove in Billy's direction?' Jesse said.

Crow let that one go.

'I came here on my own today,' Crow said. 'And we both know I wouldn't be here if I'd killed the guy. And wouldn't have been there last night if I killed the guy. Or gone to see his wife if I was planning to kill the guy.'

Jesse believed him, even if he was a killer and thief. And an enforcer. Jesse had known bad men since he'd come to Paradise from L.A., starting with Hasty Hathaway, the president of the Board of Selectmen who'd hired him, and who turned out to be a murderer himself. But none had been worse than Jimmy Macklin. Crow had worked for Macklin. Jesse would always be as wary of him as he was of Jesse. But he had done what he said he was going to do with Amber Francisco, been on the right side of that.

'You can trust me on this,' Crow said.

'Bullshit,' they both heard.

Molly walked in then.

8

She got the same jolt she had gotten in the past when in the presence of Wilson Cromartie. She refused to call it a thrill, even though she knew that's exactly what it was, at least if she was being totally honest with herself.

She still thought about him a lot. Probably too much. Cheating on Michael with him, the one and only time she had ever done that, defenseless against the urge to do it, was the worst thing she had ever done. Grandaddy of them all. The sin she knew she would take with her to her grave, one no penance, no amount of Hail Marys and Our Fathers, could get her out from under.

Devout Catholic Molly Crane.

Except for one night.

Bless me, Father, for I have sinned.

The only three people who knew about it were in Jesse's office now. Molly made sure she shut the door behind her.

'Wilson,' she said.

'Deputy Chief Crane,' Crow said. 'Is "bullshit" your standard greeting now?'

'For you it is,' she said.

She saw that all of his focus was on her. It felt like high school to her in that moment. Talking to the bad boy on whom she'd had a secret crush. But she was going to be goddamned if she was going to show him that.

Unless he could still see all the way inside of her, all the way to her secrets.

'Nice to hear you've been making friends in town,' Molly said.

'Eavesdropping?' Crow said.

'Always,' Jesse said.

Crow's face was impassive. *He changes his expression about as often as Jesse does,* Molly thought. She'd been in Crow's presence only a handful of times in her life. It just felt like more.

'So you know why I'm here,' Crow said.

'I know why you say you're here,' Molly said.

His eyes were still on her. 'Saying I'm lying?'

'Only to stay in practice.' She smiled. 'Were you practicing on Kate O'Hara?'

'You're still a bad, bad girl,' Crow said.

'Woman,' Jesse said. 'A badass woman. And second-in-command to the chief of police.' If Crow didn't notice Jesse's change in tone, the snap in his words, Molly did.

'Just reminding you to watch your mouth,' Jesse said to Crow now. 'You got history with us, Crow. But that doesn't mean you have any standing.'

Crow turned to look at him.

'Is this an official interrogation?' Crow said.

'Ask Molly,' Jesse said.

'We'll need to check your story with Kate,' she said.

'Do what you have to do,' Crow said.

'You really thought she might be able to help you with Neil?' Molly said. 'They haven't been living together for a while.'

'Like people say,' Crow said. 'Woman behind the man.'

'What people still say that?' Jesse said.

'Did you see Neil as some kind of threat to Billy's interests?' Molly said. 'Even Neil had to know he couldn't stop this thing.'

'Billy described him as being increasingly difficult,' Crow said. 'I asked his wife if she knew why. She said she didn't. I left. Now here we all are.'

'Anything else you can think of that might be helpful?' Jesse said.

'To me or you?' Crow said.

'You decide,' Jesse said.

Crow smiled again. And stood.

'We're done here,' he said.

'For now,' Jesse said.

'See you around,' Molly said.

'Look forward to it,' Crow said.

And left.

'I thought that went well,' Jesse said.

'I told you once already today,' Molly said. 'Don't start with me.'

'Furthest thing from my mind.'

'I mean it,' Molly said.

9

They were back at The Throw. Jesse had wanted to walk the scene in daylight, in case they'd missed something. He hated missing things.

'So we're not assuming it was a suicide at this point,' Suit said.

'You're aware of one of my basic rules of ace detecting, Detective,' Jesse said.

'Assume nothing.'

'There you go.'

'One of your many rules,' Suit said. 'Sometimes I think you've got more than baseball's got.'

'Not even close,' Jesse said.

Molly had a late-afternoon meeting with some church committee she was on. Her church, St. Peter's, was within walking distance of the station. Before he and Suit had left, Jesse had asked if Molly could manage not to shoot Crow if she happened to run into him on the street. She said she wasn't promising anything.

'Dev says there's nothing to indicate that if somebody else did shoot him, that they dumped the body here, right?' Suit said.

'Doesn't mean it didn't happen that way,' Jesse said.

Jesse mentioned to Suit again about the only residue being on O'Hara's right hand.

'Been thinking about that,' Suit said. 'But there are guys who play ball left-handed and write with their right hands.'

'Or the guy who shot him didn't know Neil was left-handed, and just put the gun in his right hand,' Jesse said. 'And by the way? Neil wrote with his left hand.'

'You already checked it out,' Suit said. 'Of course you did.'

'You think they let just anybody be chief?' Jesse said.

Jesse loved Suitcase Simpson, had from the first time he'd met him as an overeager kid. He was smart, tough, loyal. And now that he'd married Elena, he'd stopped trying to screw his way through Paradise, Mass.

Jesse treated him like a son even though he had a real son in Cole Slayton, one he didn't know about until a couple years ago. Cole had tried the cops. He was now in his first year of law school, Loyola Marymount, back in Los Angeles, where he'd been raised by his mother. For now he was planning to specialize in financial crimes, saying he was tired of rich assholes finding ways to keep all the money.

Jesse and Suit had started out by walking the perimeter again, slowly making their way back to the grave in which Jesse had found Neil O'Hara.

'Who do you think is going to end up with the land?' Suit said.

'No clue.'

'You got a preference?'

'Yeah, that the land stays protected,' Jesse said. 'I need a casino in our town like I need a hole in the head.'

Suit said, 'You think that if Neil did kill himself, he was trying to tell us something by doing it here?'

'I don't believe he killed himself,' Jesse said.

'Whose side was Neil on?' Suit said.

'My opinion? He was a tree hugger at heart and hated both of them.'

'But if he was leaning toward one of them, Singer or Barrone, knowing he'd have to choose,' Suit said, 'would the other one have him killed?'

'Guys like them, rich as they are, are like the rest of us,' Jesse said. 'Get up in the morning, go to bed at night. Except in between, nobody gets to say no to them. But the good news for them is that now they've got a new mayor practically in heat to say yes.'

Jesse felt his phone buzzing, took it out of the side pocket of his windbreaker.

'Speak of the devil,' Jesse said.

'Woof,' Suit said.

10

Molly had told Jesse once that Gary Armistead reminded her of Justin Timberlake. Jesse had asked her who Justin Timberlake was. It was one of those conversations involving any kind of modern culture that always ended with Molly telling him she didn't know why she even tried.

Early thirties, lots of brown hair piled up on top and what looked to be a lot of product in it, deep-fried tan. There may have been more eligible bachelors in Paradise, but Jesse couldn't think of one off the top of his head.

Word around town was that Armistead, with a lot of family money behind him, had his eyes on the congressional district in which Paradise was situated, that seat opening up in a year and a half when the current holder of the office finally retired after about a dozen terms. Jesse was of the opinion that only some kind of vaccine could make Armistead's ambition less toxic than it already was.

He made Jesse come to him the next day. The Board of Selectmen offices now took up the top floor of the converted firehouse on Broad Street. There was just enough of a view for them to see the tops of boats in the harbor.

Armistead, Jesse discovered when he got there, had already moved into Neil O'Hara's old office.

'I know what you're probably thinking,' Armistead said when Jesse sat down across from him.

'Somehow I doubt that,' Jesse said.

'But I asked Kate if she had any objections to me moving in here,' he said. 'She didn't. So you shouldn't. Neil was my friend.'

Jesse thought, *In a pig's eye he was.*

Armistead had yanked down his tie. Now he leaned back in

what had been Neil O'Hara's chair and put his feet up on what had been Neil's desk. Clasped his hands behind his head.

'I'm hoping we can have the same kind of solid working relationship that you and Neil had,' Armistead said.

'I'm easy,' Jesse said.

Armistead smiled. 'Well, we both know that's a crock.'

'Gary,' Jesse said, 'why don't you tell me why I'm here, so our working relationship can involve me actually working.'

Armistead took his feet off the desk, pulled the chair closer to it, leaned forward, smile gone.

'I'd like you to cut the shit on "maybe it's a suicide and maybe it's not,"' he said. 'You know Ellis Munroe feels the same way, for chrissakes.'

'My investigation into Neil's death isn't even twenty-four hours old,' Jesse said. 'Jumping to conclusions, or drawing any, is for amateurs at this point.'

'We need to move past this,' Armistead said.

'As soon as I determine what happened to him,' Jesse said.

Another guy who didn't like being told no, Jesse thought. You could see it in his eyes, so pale Jesse couldn't tell whether they were blue or green.

'I'm not Neil,' he said. 'Meaning I'm not the kind of boss looking to hug things out.'

Jesse grinned. 'There's a relief.'

'You don't like me very much, do you, Chief?'

'Doesn't matter whether I do or don't,' Jesse said. 'You *are* my boss now.'

'Who's telling you to wrap this thing up as quickly as possible,' Armistead said. 'Even though he's gone, this land deal is going to be Neil's legacy, whether he was behind it or not. And this town needs it.'

'When I determine if this was a suicide or not, you'll be the first to know.'

Armistead said, 'So we're back there.'

'Never left,' Jesse said.

'You really think somebody killed Neil?' Armistead said. 'Or had him killed?'

'We've got two powerful men who hate each other's guts fighting for something they both want,' Jesse said.

'Jesus,' Armistead said, 'you're going to treat them like *suspects*?'

'No.'

'Thank the Lord.'

'*Persons of interest* would be more like it,' Jesse said.

'For something that we both know is going to turn out to be a suicide in the end.'

'You sound as if wishing might make it so.'

'You're smart enough to know how this plays out if you go out of your way to muck up this deal,' Armistead said.

'You'll have my badge?' Jesse said.

'Is that your idea of irony?' Armistead said.

'Trying to quit,' he said.

'Like drinking?' Armistead said.

'Drinking might have been easier, now that I think about it.'

'I *will* fire you,' Gary Armistead said.

And there it is.

'Understood,' Jesse said.

Armistead came around the desk now, letting Jesse know that the meeting was over, and that he was being dismissed.

Jesse stood.

'Until Neil came along, I can't tell you how many people who've had your job have told me they were going to fire me,' he said.

He remembered something Crow had said earlier.

'And yet,' Jesse said, 'here I am.'

11

Jesse was still in his office at seven o'clock. Some days he was headed home by now. But not many. The nights alone were getting longer and longer with Sunny away. Cole was experiencing, in real time, what the first year of law school was really like, which meant boot camp.

'You ever feel outgunned?' he'd said to his father the last time they'd talked.

'Never,' Jesse had told him.

'When Mom was alive she wanted me to be a lawyer and not a cop,' he said. 'You think she knows I'm finally doing it? The lawyer thing, I mean?'

'She always knew everything,' Jesse said. 'No reason for her to change course now.'

'Damn, this shit is hard,' Cole said.

'Head down,' Jesse said, 'eyes up.'

He finally walked outside and got into the Explorer, drove home, turned on the television, the Sox game against the Rays just starting. He wondered if this would be one of the nights when he'd still be awake by the time the game ended. As much as he loved baseball, as much as he knew it would always be in his DNA, even he could watch only so much of it, especially the way the Sox had played the first couple months of the season.

He went into the kitchen, thinking he would pan-fry a steak, throw some mushrooms on it, bake himself a potato.

Then he was opening the cupboard where he'd always kept the scotch, thinking of all the nights when baseball and scotch were all the company he needed, until he wasn't awake for the end of the game because he was passed out drunk.

Maybe what he really needed tonight was a meeting. He hadn't been to one in a couple weeks.

'It's when you drop your guard,' Dix said, 'that you get tagged so hard you end up on Queer Street.'

'Not sure they still call it that,' Jesse said. 'Obvious reasons.'

'Queer Street by any other name,' Dix said.

Jesse didn't want a drink tonight. He didn't get the urge every night. Not even most. Just some. Sometimes the urge was stronger than at other times. He stood and stared into the empty cupboard.

In his mind, the bottle was always there.

He imagined himself uncapping it now, Dewar's or Johnnie Walker or whatever it was, checking to see how much was in there, telling himself that tonight was finally going to be the one when he learned how to pace himself, even drinking alone. Deciding whether to mix it with soda or just splash some over ice.

My amber waves, he used to think.

He shook his head now, shaking himself out of his reverie, making a plan for himself, a checklist, knowing he wanted to talk to Lawton and Singer and Barrone, and the other members of the Board, ask them if they'd noticed anything unusual about Neil O'Hara's behavior lately. Had they seen the signs of depression that Kate had talked about? Had any of them ever heard him mention a gun? When was the last time any of them had spoken to him? Do it by the numbers.

He would decide on the order in which he wanted to talk to all the players in the game tomorrow. For now he watched the Red Sox, not falling asleep one time. He was wide awake when it ended around eleven, another modern ballgame that had gone on far too long.

He picked up his phone and called Sunny.

She answered right away.

'If you start heavy breathing,' she said, 'I'm calling the police.'

'I am the police,' he said.

'You must need help fighting crime,' she said.

'Maybe I just miss you,' he said.

45

'I thought we weren't going to do this.'

'Miss each other?'

'Call when we did.'

There was a silence so long that Jesse checked the screen of his phone to make sure they were still connected.

He could hear voices in the background.

'Where are you?' he said.

'Out to dinner,' she said, and left it at that. He let her leave it at that.

'Aren't you up late, Chief?' she said.

It was as if she were changing the subject, though Jesse frankly wasn't sure what the subject was.

He told her about Neil O'Hara, about him being left-handed, about the angle of the bullet, about him having gotten himself sideways with Singer and Barrone.

'You don't think the guy killed himself.'

'Do not.'

'But you can't officially rule it out,' she said.

'Cannot.'

'I see you're as chatty as ever, Chief Stone.'

'Been a while since we talked,' he said. 'I could be out of practice.'

'It'll come back to you,' she said. 'Like riding a bike.'

'You sure?' he said.

Another silence, longer than before.

'How's your case going?' Jesse said.

'They lie a lot out here,' Sunny said.

'I could have told you,' Jesse said.

'Listen,' she said, 'I've got to get back to the table. I'll call when we have more time.'

I've actually got all the time in the world.

She ended the call before he did. He shut off the postgame show and the lights in the living room and took one more look out at the ocean, just to make sure it was still there.

He walked into his second bedroom, the one where Cole

slept when he'd stay the night, and opened the middle drawer and pulled out the napkin.

12

The napkin from Daisy Dyke's had one word written on it, uppercase letters, underlined for emphasis:

<u>NEVER</u>

It had been Jesse's last breakfast with Neil O'Hara the week before he died, and Jesse, looking back, felt badly about it now, because he'd invited Neil only to lobby him to put more money for the department into the upcoming budget, even knowing how the town's economy was still suffering the aftershocks of COVID-19.

It was why more people in town than not, a lot more, wanted the land deal to pass the Board with flying colors.

'Think of this as a soft sell,' Jesse had said that day.

Neil had grinned and said, 'There's no such thing with you.'

'I've wanted to add a couple more cops for a few years,' Jesse said.

'And I'd like this thing with The Throw to magically disappear,' he said.

'Why they pay you the big bucks,' Jesse said.

Neil had lowered his voice and said, 'The big bucks are the ones I've been offered by both Singer and Barrone to get behind this in public more than I have. Get more locals on board.'

'You're just one vote out of five, correct?' Jesse said. 'When it comes time to decide.'

'Lawton and Singer and Barrone don't seem to see it that

way,' he said. 'They think I have more power than I do to influence the other members of the Board.'

'Because people respect you.'

Neil grinned again. 'You're not getting the two cops.'

Jesse remembered now how tired he looked. Kate had talked about him being worn down.

'I just want it to be over,' Neil said.

Jesse had leaned forward then, motioning for Neil to do the same, lowering his own voice.

'I want to ask you a question, even if I think I already know the answer,' he said. 'And I won't quote you.'

'The last person in town who has to make that assurance is you,' Neil said.

Keeping his voice low, Jesse said, 'I know how you feel about the land in this town, and not just the land we're talking about. But we both know how the money in this thing, even if we think it's dirty money, will help stand Paradise up again.'

'It doesn't even matter what *I* think any longer,' Neil said. 'It's a five-person Board. There are three votes in favor locked in, unless somebody changes their mind. The only dissenting vote is Constance Burden, whose family even beat the pilgrims here.'

Jesse sat at his desk now, remembering all over again what he had said next.

'You're going to have to run for reelection one of these days,' Jesse said. 'And you know you can't stop the thing. Any chance you might go along just to get along, just in the interest of self-preservation?'

Neil had smiled at Jesse then, took a pen out of the inside pocket of his sports jacket, and wrote <u>NEVER</u> on his napkin, slid it across the table to Jesse, then slid out of his seat and told Jesse he'd pay their bill at the register. He didn't seem depressed that day, Jesse thought to himself now. Just boxed in by events he couldn't do anything to stop.

Jesse stared at the napkin again. He'd been doing it a lot, as if he were looking at Neil O'Hara's last will and testament.

He didn't have the power to kill the deal, but somebody had killed him anyway.

But who?

And why?

13

He was in his office late the next afternoon, having had no success across the day contacting Lawton or Singer or Barrone, when Suit walked in, grinning.

'There's an SOB here to see you,' he said.

'Not the first time,' Jesse said. 'Certainly won't be the last.'

'I mean one of the tree huggers,' Suit said. 'She's pretty upset. Says her boyfriend has disappeared.'

'Who's her boyfriend?'

'The head hugger.'

The young woman's name was Blair Richmond. She was tall and blonde and could have been a younger sister to Jesse's ex-wife, Jenn. Her boyfriend's name was Ben Gage, whom she said had founded SOB when Thomas Lawton put the land up for sale.

Blair Richmond said she'd spent the past few days visiting an old friend in Providence. Jesse asked if she had any family. She said no, that she was an only child and both her parents had passed. She said Ben was her family now, but that when she got back to the house in Paradise she shared with him, in a section of town near the Marshport line known as the Lost District, it had been searched, top to bottom.

'Do you have any idea what might have been taken?' Jesse said. 'Or anything Ben might have been hiding?'

She shook her head.

'I wouldn't even know where to begin,' she said. 'Everything was everywhere.'

'And you have no idea where Ben is,' Jesse said.

'He could be *any*where,' she said.

He sat behind his desk. She paced, her nervous energy almost having built to being kinetic. She had tattoos up and down both bare arms, ear piercings, a nose ring. Maybe Ben Gage thought it made her more beautiful, and made him start to yearn for exclusivity. Jesse knew it was generational, not understanding tats or the piercings. Just more things on the list of things he didn't understand about people her age, like preferring text messaging to actual conversation.

Jesse said, 'Do you and Ben work together?'

'I work with him and believe in him,' she said.

'Have you actually helped him dig the graves?'

Her eyes narrowed. 'Are you going to arrest me if I tell you that I have?'

'No.'

'Sometimes,' she said. 'My dad was a mason. I made most of the headstones, even the ones we have stored because we haven't used them yet.'

'In what way?'

'Mr Lawton has security now,' she said. 'Not all the time. Sometimes. Last week Ben and I had just finished putting a headstone in place when a man pulled up on the access road in some kind of Jeep. He was too far away for me to get a good look at him. But Ben and I took off when he started running in our direction.'

'You did get away, though?'

'We had a good head start, and made our way down through the bluffs to the beach,' she said. 'I told Ben that should be our last grave. He said maybe I was right, he was worried that he was being followed lately.'

She stopped in front of his desk. 'You don't think we're criminals?'

He smiled. 'I sometimes get the urge to grab a shovel and head over there with you,' Jesse said. 'And if you repeat that, I *will* arrest you.'

She sat down now.

'When was the last time you actually did hear from him?' Jesse said.

'He called me the night Mr O'Hara died,' she said, 'for like a minute. Maybe less. I'd just gotten to my friend's house. He was using another burner phone, which was all he'd been using lately. Said he didn't have much time. I asked what was going on. He said a lot. He said he'd come up with something that was going to change everything for him and Mr O'Hara. I asked what. He said he didn't have enough time to tell me everything he needed to tell me on the phone. And he was worried that somebody might be listening. I love him so much, but sometimes he acts as if we're in some kind of spy movie.'

'That was it?'

'That's what he told me, pretty much word for word,' she said. 'But like I just told you, it was pretty rushed.'

'He hasn't tried to reach out since?'

'That's what scares me, Mr Stone,' she said. 'If whatever he came up with *was* so important, I keep thinking he would have reached back out to me, unless something bad has happened to him. The other kids in SOB haven't heard from him, either. I asked if he'd told any of them anything. He hadn't. Even though we all helped out, SOB was really Ben in the end. We all got caught up in it because of him. But it was Ben who was the true believer. He was obsessed with doing whatever he had to do to stop this deal from going through.'

She reached into the bag lying next to her chair and pulled out one of those vape pens and sucked on it like it was a pacifier.

One more thing to add to the list of things he didn't understand, to go with the tats and piercings, Jesse thought.

'Ben hated that I used this,' she said. 'It was like he was out of another time. He just loves nature so much. He even likes being

51

called a tree hugger. He wondered what the people calling him that would say if they knew he'd built us this cool treehouse in the backyard, the one in front of their wishing tree. We sit up there at night sometimes and dream about our kids sitting up in it someday.'

Jesse thought she might cry.

'There's such a sweetness about him, as much as he tries to come across as a tough guy,' she said. 'He used to leave love letters for me and just wait for me to find them.'

Bring her back, Jesse told himself.

'Is there anything else you can remember that he said that night?' he said.

'He could be dead!' Blair said.

'Maybe he's just hiding out until he thinks it's safe to come back,' Jesse said. 'Maybe he really was being followed.'

'He tries to act as if he's not afraid of them,' she said, 'but he sounded so geeked the night he called.'

'"Them" meaning Singer and Barrone?'

'All of them,' she said. 'Mr Lawton ran into Ben in town last week, after we got chased, and told him that if we didn't stop trespassing, he'd be sorry. Said that next time his guys would catch us.'

'He said that?'

'Word for word,' she said. 'He's no better than the other two, if you ask me.'

She stared at the vape pen, and sadly shook her head.

'No blue light,' she said. 'Means it's empty.'

'Good to know,' Jesse said.

'Ben should have called by now!'

He told her he would send a couple of his people over to her house to check it for evidence, and then lock it down until further notice. He asked if there was someone with whom she could stay for a couple days. She said there was another couple in the group who could take her in. Sam and Diane Burrows. They lived over in Marshport.

'This is all because of what happened to Mr O'Hara, isn't it?' she said.

'It seems to be what we call a "precipitating event,"' Jesse said.

'Ben really liked him, Mr O'Hara. He never came out and said it in public, but Ben felt he was with us one hundred percent. Ben didn't trust the police anymore, all due respect, because of everything that's been happening in the country. But he did trust Mr O'Hara.'

Jesse told her to contact him immediately if she heard from Ben. She said she would.

'You have to find him,' she said to Jesse. '*Please* find him,' she said.

Jesse asked if she had a car. She said she'd walked here from their house. Jesse said he could have someone drive her back there. She said she wanted to walk, that she used long walks to meditate sometimes.

'Hey, I forgot one thing,' Blair said after Jesse had walked her through the front room. 'Someone else came by the house a few days ago, before Ben disappeared, wanting to talk to him.'

Jesse waited.

'He was this kind of scary Native American man,' she said.

14

Jesse and Molly and Suit were back in Jesse's office after Blair Richmond left. Before she had, she'd spent some time talking to Molly at her desk. Molly said she'd given Blair her phone number, and told her to call if she needed anything.

'I assume you're going to talk to Crow about him paying a call on those kids,' Molly said.

'Be practically criminal not to,' Jesse said.

'You think Crow might have something to do with Ben being in the wind?' Suit said.

'"In the wind," Suit?' Jesse said. 'Seriously?'

'I watch too many cop shows,' he said.

'What I think,' Jesse said, 'is that some do-gooding kids ended up way over their heads, with people even worse than they thought they were coming into this.'

'I saw that girl walk in,' Molly said. 'She could be one of my daughters. All on fire with saving the world.'

'Like their mother,' Jesse said.

Jesse had planned on paying a visit to Thomas Lawton, who had stopped returning his calls. Not calling first this time. Just show up at his house and brace him on threatening Ben Gage, who had now disappeared. And ask about his private security chasing people off land that had been protected by his family for years until he was in control of it. Molly once called Lawton the second-biggest asshole in Paradise, Mass. When Jesse asked her why just the second, Molly said she just assumed there was a bigger one they all hadn't met yet.

When Jesse was alone in his office he reached into the drawer below his gun drawer and once again pulled out his baseball glove, the one he'd been wearing when his career had ended in Albuquerque. Almost like it was a comforter.

Cole had somehow found an exact replica of the glove, and given it to him as a gift. But the one on his left hand now was the real thing. Sometimes it helped him clear his head and think.

Neil O'Hara and Ben Gage, one the mayor, one the official head of the opposition, had been a part of the story from the start. So had Thomas Lawton, who'd started all the action in the first place, when he'd decided to sell the land, and brought Billy Singer and Ed Barrone into it, and into Paradise. Neil O'Hara had now died on that land. Ben Gage had gone missing after telling his girlfriend that he had come up with something that could change everything.

Jesse snapped the ball into his glove.

Now Crow kept wandering in and out of the story. He had been at The Throw that night. He admitted to having seen Neil O'Hara's wife a few hours before. And, as it turned out, had come knocking on Ben Gage's door wanting to chat before *that*.

Jesse put his glove and ball back in the drawer. It took him two phone calls to locate the address of Crow's Airbnb. It was on Grove Street. Three blocks from where Ben Gage and Blair Richmond lived in the Lost District. Maybe something else that wasn't a coincidence.

Time to go have another chat with the scary Native American man.

Not necessarily going in peace.

Jesse didn't really need to put the address in Waze. He did anyway, just so he could go straight to the right house.

18 Grove.

Molly's car was out front when he got there.

15

Jesse didn't slow down, just kept going down Grove to Forest Avenue, where he made a turn that might have been classified as illegal if the one making it wasn't the chief of police.

Then he pulled up at the corner of Grove and Forest with a clear view of 18 Grove and reviewed his limited options, none of which he considered great at the moment.

He could drive back up the street and do what he'd come over here to do, and question Crow. But if he did that, just walked up and rang the bell or knocked on the front door, Molly would likely think he was checking up on her, like an overprotective father. Or a boss who had specifically told her to stay away from Wilson Cromartie.

Maybe she was just following up on what Blair Richmond

had told Jesse about Crow having come calling. And if Jesse showed up, it would appear, in the best possible light, as if he wasn't allowing Molly to do her job and handle this on her own.

Whether he'd told her to stay away from Crow or not.

He sat in the Explorer and waited. He was good at it. Waiting. It was past six o'clock by now, the time between the end of the afternoon and the beginning of evening, the sky gone dark, the wind suddenly at a howl, announcing the imminent arrival of a storm the way the black clouds over the ocean had done the exact same thing over the past hour, the kind of storm, Jesse knew, that was like a message that there was an occasional bill presented for living in a setting like this, and for everyone to be ready when it came due.

Then the rain was all around him, followed by explosions of thunder and lightning, the force of the wind already making Jesse worry about power outages and downed trees and wires in the night ahead.

He turned on his wipers and felt the Explorer shake and thought about Molly Crane, hoping that she was at the rented house only on police business, and not personal. She had sworn to Jesse, every time the subject of Crow had come up over the years, that what had happened between them would never happen again, with him or anybody else, that she would never again cheat on Michael, that she wouldn't risk her marriage a second time.

Jesse believed her. Maybe it was because he wanted to believe her. And maybe because there was no other person in his life, not Sunny, not even his own son, about whom he cared more, for whom he wanted only good things.

But perhaps her vow about Crow was easy to make because she never thought she would see him again, that when he'd left Paradise the last time he'd left for good.

And yet here he was.

Here she was.

Here were they all.

She was Jesse's best friend. In so many ways, all the big ways, she was the best friend he'd ever had in his life. She had saved his job more than once. And maybe his life. Molly Crane: friend, deputy, wife, mother.

Somehow the wind was blowing even harder from the east than it was before. More lightning exploded, feeling closer than ever, as if it had targeted Grove Street. More thunder followed, shaking the Explorer again.

Molly Crane, halfway down the block with Crow.

He sat there for another half hour and then finally put the Explorer in gear, took a left on Grove, away from the rented house, and headed for home. Thinking this might be one of those nights when he wanted a drink more than others.

Perfect storm.

16

Molly sat curled up at one end of her living room couch, one which she and Michael had sometimes put to rocking good use, on the rare occasions when they'd had the house to themselves when the girls were still around, and then after they weren't.

She poured herself a glass of chardonnay.

She had just been alone with Crow for the first time since she'd slept with him, though without making too fine a point of things, they hadn't done any sleeping that night.

'This couldn't wait?' Crow had said when he opened the door and saw her standing there.

'No,' Molly had said, walking past and into the small, spare front room without being invited in. Like she was *taking* the room, even if she didn't feel that way at all.

Fake it till you make it.

'Is this an official visit?' Crow said.

Molly's throat was dry, but she didn't want to clear it, as if even that might be a sign of weakness, or nerves. Or both. One of her guilty pleasures – an innocent one – was country music. And one of her favorite singers was Delbert McClinton, who once sang about old weaknesses, comin' on strong.

Crow sat on the sofa. Molly took a chair across from him, facing him across a cheap coffee table trying to look as if it were made of mahogany.

Crow grinned.

'So how can I help you?' he said.

Everything he said to her sounded as if it had subtext. Or just a double meaning.

He's enjoying this.

'Ben Gage has disappeared,' she said.

'Who's that?'

'Let's not,' Molly said.

Her voice sounded husky to her, nothing she could do about it now.

'Not what?'

'Fuck around.'

She was sorry as soon as she said it.

Crow grinned again. 'You sure about that?'

'We can do this here,' Molly said. 'Or I can call Jesse and have him meet us at the station. Your call.'

He jerked a thumb in the direction of the tiny kitchen that was like an extension of the room. 'Get you something?'

'I won't be here long enough,' Molly said.

'It's good to see you again,' Crow said.

'*You* sure about that?' she said.

She felt as if the room were shrinking, as if he could reach across the coffee table and have his hands on her before she could do anything to stop him. If she wanted to stop him. She had disabled her phone before she'd left the station. Perhaps the only person who knew where she was at this moment was Crow.

'Why did you go to Ben Gage's house?' she said.

'I wanted to know if he and his little green men were going to continue to bust balls if Billy got the land,' he said.

'Men and women,' Molly said.

Crow gave a quick shake of his head. 'Whatever,' he said.

'Why couldn't you just ask the young woman he lives with?' she said.

'He's the boss,' Crow said. 'You just spin your wheels talking to someone who's not the boss.'

'You feel as if you're wasting your time not talking to *my* boss?' Molly said.

'By now,' Crow said, 'I know that talking to you is the same as talking to him.'

Another bolt of lightning rattled the windows at 18 Grove. It made Molly jump.

'Don't worry,' Crow said. 'I'll protect you.'

Molly smiled. 'If you're lying to us about any of this, you're the one who will need protection,' she said. 'Unless you've got another getaway boat waiting.'

'I got nothing to do with the dead guy,' he said. 'I got nothing to do with this Ben Gage disappearing.'

'So you say.'

'Let me ask you something,' Crow said to her. 'Are we ever going to get past this?'

'This,' Molly said.

He made a gesture that seemed to take in the two of them, and the space in between.

Molly said, 'I got past it a long time ago.' She shrugged. 'Regrets, I've had a few.'

Crow said, 'Now who's lying?'

'Don't flatter yourself.'

Then she said, 'Does Billy Singer want this land enough to kill for it?'

'You mean have me kill for it, don't you?'

Molly's shoulders rose and fell again.

'He might kill Ed Barrone if he thought he could get away with it,' Crow said. 'Not anybody else. But if you and the chief want to treat me like a suspect, have at it.' He grinned again and put up his palm. 'Your chief, white woman. Not mine.'

Molly had left then, feeling the urge to run through the rain to the old Cherokee that she refused to give up or trade in, even though Jesse told her she was entitled to the same kind of Explorer he drove.

She drove home slowly through some streets that were already flooded. Took a shower. Built the fire. Wondering what it was like for Michael out on the ocean, wherever he was on the ocean, when a storm like this would hit in the night and there was nowhere to hide, nothing between you and the sky. Or God.

She realized that she had forgotten to turn her phone back on. She grabbed it out of her bag and did now. There was another missed call from Jesse, one that had come in while she was in the shower. He'd also called earlier in the evening.

She decided she would call him back in the morning. Looked at her glass and realized she had barely touched her wine. She took the glass into the kitchen and poured the wine into the sink. Then she got the keys to the Cherokee out of her bag and headed outside. The rain had stopped.

She thought about another Delbert song now, the one about some kind of crazy.

17

Molly was late getting to the station the next morning. If she wasn't on an assignment, she was usually only late for some kind of family situation. But Jesse knew she had no family in town these days. Her daughters were all grown and out of the house, and her husband was still out on the Atlantic Ocean somewhere. He'd asked Michael Crane whether he loved Molly more, or sailing.

'Molly,' Michael Crane had said. 'But it's a close call.'

Jesse had tried Molly's phone the night before, once after he'd gotten home from Crow's, once later. She had not called him back, something she routinely did, no matter the time of day or night. The last time he had known her whereabouts had been when she was on Grove Street, at Crow's rented house, before he had driven away.

When she finally arrived a few minutes after ten, she had her phone in her hand and was waving it at Jesse.

'I just tried to call Blair Richmond at her friends' house,' she said. 'No answer. Then I called the friends. She never showed up there last night.'

'Son of a bitch,' he said.

'My sentiments exactly.'

'Something must have spooked her now,' Jesse said.

'Or she heard from her boyfriend and went to meet up with him.'

'We've got her phone number,' Jesse said. 'We could track her with that.'

'On it,' Molly said. 'But I bet if she was worried about being tracked, she knew how to pull the battery out of the phone and then only put it back when she wanted to use it.'

'No matter how tech-savvy we think we are, kids are savvier,' Jesse said.

'I'll check anything and everything,' Molly said. 'And then see about credit cards or debit cards and social media and all that jazz, whether she's gone to ground or not. But if she wants to go off the grid, maybe she's smart enough to pay for everything in cash.'

'I should have checked in with her last night,' Jesse said.

'One of us should have,' Molly said. 'I took a ride over to their house instead, just on the chance somebody might have taken another run at it.'

'You mean you took a ride over without telling me,' Jesse said.

'Am I required to?' she said.

He took off his reading glasses. He was using them more and more, because if he didn't, he needed to move whatever he was reading farther and farther away. What had they called doing that when he was a kid? Playing the trombone?

Playing the trombone?

Jesus, how old am I?

He knew he wasn't angry with Molly. He was angry about a lot of things these days. Including Sunny. But Molly was the only one here right now.

'What time did you go over there?' Jesse said.

'Are we really going to do this?' she said. 'What does it matter?'

Maybe she was reading his mind, something she did with consistent ease. She got up out of her chair now and walked over to his door and shut it and sat back down.

'It's just that I tried to call *you* last night,' Jesse said. 'Usually I hear back when you see a missed call from me.'

He drank some coffee and decided to stop screwing around.

'You went to see Crow,' he said.

They both knew it wasn't a question. She waited a beat, eyes on him, before answering.

'Did he tell you that?'

'He didn't have to,' Jesse said. 'I saw your car in front of his house.'

'You *followed* me?' she said. 'What the hell, Jesse?'

'I was following up on what Blair Richmond had told me,' he said.

'Are we done talking about her?'

'I'll get back to her,' Jesse said. 'Just taking the circle route.'

'*I* was following up on her telling us that Crow had gone to their house,' Molly said. '*Did* I need a hall pass?'

'You know better than that.'

'I was there as a cop,' she said. 'Nothing else. *Okay?*'

She stepped on the last word.

'I just want to make sure you're okay,' he said.

'Did I ask you if you were okay after you went to see your old girlfriend the night that Neil died?' Molly said.

'You did not.'

Molly said, 'Then you don't have to worry about me.'

'A chronic condition, unfortunately.'

'Get over it.'

'Trust me, I've tried. I wasn't following you,' Jesse said before Molly left the office.

'If you say so.'

'I say so because I really wasn't following you. Okay?'

'Okay.'

She stopped at his door, hand on the knob.

'Change of subject?'

Jesse said, 'I'd be willing to pay big bucks for one.'

'Why were you so sure it was murder with Neil from the start?' she said.

'Too many things didn't add up,' he said. 'Him using his off hand. Dev was the first one to say the angle of the bullet, even if he was right-handed, was off.'

'Now we've got two missing kids,' Molly said.

'Had one of them right here in this office,' Jesse said. 'Let her walk right out the door.'

'But she told you that she didn't know anything,' Molly said.

'We know that,' Jesse said. 'They don't.'

'Whoever they are,' Molly said.

'She told me to find her boyfriend,' Jesse said. 'Now I want you to find her.'

She managed a smile.

'You know what you always tell me,' she said.

'I tell you a lot of things,' he said. 'Unfortunately, you seem to remember most of them.'

'If this shit were easy,' Molly said, 'anybody would do it.'

Jesse said it ought to be a Hallmark card.

18

Billy Singer might not have been the most famous casino owner in Vegas. If he wasn't, he was definitely in the conversation. It was mostly because of his television commercials for the centerpiece of his gaming empire, one that included casinos in Tahoe and London, simply known as The House.

'Come to Las Vegas,' Billy would say, looking into the camera, 'and see if you can take my money home with you. Everybody thinks they can beat The House. Come see us, and see if you can beat mine.'

He reminded Jesse of the old actor George Hamilton. But then the only actors Jesse knew were old ones. White hair, perpetually dark tan, admitting to being seventy-two now but older than that according to internet biographies, looking a lot younger than that up close because of all the expert work he'd clearly had done. Only his veiny hands betrayed him, because they always did. *Hands got you every time,* Jesse thought. He was frankly amazed that Singer had allowed his hair to go snow white, that he wasn't one of those aging celebrities with hair the color of one of his baseball mitts.

Singer had rented a big place on Stiles Island for the duration of his competition with Ed Barrone. Singer said he planned to buy a place of his own, or build one, once he was awarded the land. 'When,' he always said, not 'if.' Like a guy running for office and saying, *when* I'm elected. Like it was some kind of sure thing.

Singer answered the door himself. Lime-green polo shirt, skinny jeans, expensive-looking boat shoes. Firm handshake, as if he'd learned it at Big Guy school.

'Whatever it is, I didn't do it,' he said, leading Jesse into a massive living room with high ceilings and lots of windows and a panoramic view of the water, with the Stiles Island Bridge off to his right. Somewhere in the vast distance was Portugal, or The Azores; Jesse could never remember which came first.

As good as the view was from here, Jesse knew the view from The Throw, up much higher, was even better.

Billy Singer jerked his head in the direction of an impressively stocked bar.

'Get you a drink, Chief?' Singer said. He smiled. 'It's five o'clock somewhere, right?'

'Maybe you haven't heard,' Jesse said. 'I retired with the trophy.'

One of his stock lines. He didn't attend many cocktail parties. Rarely attended parties of any kind, really. But when he did, and somebody would offer him a drink, he'd simply say, 'I've already had enough.'

'Did I know that?' Singer said. 'Shit, I hope it's not one more thing I forgot. Every time I can't find the damn remote, I think I'm on my way to getting diagnosed with the big Al.'

They sat in a sun-splashed area at the end of the room that opened out onto a deck. Singer was working on a Bloody Mary. Jesse idly wondered if it was his first of the day.

'So how can I help you?' Singer said.

'You could start by telling me why you thought you needed to bring in Crow to close a real estate transaction,' Jesse said.

'You know Crow?' Singer said.

'You know Crow and I have history, Billy,' Jesse said. 'And you know that I know that you know, because it's something Crow would have told you before he ever got to town.' Jesse smiled. 'This will go a lot easier if you don't try to bullshit me like you're one of your casino hosts instead of the guy who owns the place.'

Singer's smile held. But by threads.

'Little aggressive there, am I right?'

Jesse was still smiling back at him. 'Not even close.'

'You know about casino hosts?' Singer said.

'And used-car salesmen,' Jesse said. 'And guys selling steak knives when I'm up too late watching television.'

Singer laughed.

'Not a fan of Vegas, I'm guessing?' Singer said.

'Not even close,' Jesse said again.

'I'm not here selling,' Singer said. 'Just trying to buy.'

'Why do you want the land this much?'

'Now, just for the sake of conversation, what if I were to tell you that my business is none of yours?'

'Would make me wonder about your business even more,' Jesse said, 'and if that had anything to do with the death of Neil O'Hara.'

'That's *your* business,' Singer said.

'I'm just trying to understand yours,' Jesse said.

'I want this deal for the same reason I want everything,' he said. 'Because I do. Because I already own as much of the Strip as I'm going to own. Because I have been looking to expand to this part of the country for a while, especially now that you don't have to be in a tribe to own a casino here.'

Jesse watched him closely as he listened. And despite all the spit-shine to him, all the teeth and hair and what he was certain was killer charm, Jesse could see the predator in the man, like a hawk making a high, slow pass.

'How much of this has to do with the fact that Ed Barrone wants what you want, too?' Jesse said.

Singer grabbed the celery stalk out of his drink and ate half of it. 'Well,' he said, 'there is that.'

'Why do you hate him so much?'

'That bindle stiff isn't important enough to hate,' Singer said. 'He's just somebody in the way before you win and he loses.'

'I read he made a run at you a year or two after you first opened your casino,' Jesse said.

'I'd hit a rough patch,' Singer said. 'I came out of it, despite the fake news on that.' He shrugged. 'It's what I do. But before I did, he came at me with friends of his who were enemies of mine.'

'Guessing that's not something that would be easy to forget.'

'When I'm dead,' Billy Singer said. 'And maybe not even then.'

'This land worth killing for?' Jesse said.

'You asking about him, or me?'

'Either way.'

'Him,' Singer said. 'Not me. That was the old Vegas. Like the one in the movies. Not mine.'

Jesse got up and walked to the window and stared out at the ocean. When he turned around he said, 'A couple of kids who've been digging those graves at The Throw have disappeared. Any chance you know anything about that?'

'I've got nothing to do with any of that,' he said. 'That's Lawton's problem, for as long as it's still his land. When it's mine, I'll deal with them if they keep it up.'

'Crow went to see one of the kids,' Jesse said. 'Any idea why?'

'Ask Crow,' Singer said. He smiled and showed Jesse a lot of teeth even whiter than his hair. 'Listen, here's all you have to know about me. I'm just a guy trying to buy some prime real estate. You don't need to treat me like some grifter on the hustle.'

'Your words,' Jesse said, 'not mine.'

'I got a gift for reading people,' Singer said.

When they got to the door, he shook Jesse's hand again, even more firmly than before. Jesse waited until he was behind the wheel of the Explorer before counting his fingers.

He was on his way back to the station when Suit called and told him Molly was at Urgent Care.

'Why?' Jesse said.

'Somebody knocked her out over at the tree huggers' house,' Suit said. He paused. 'One punch.'

He paused and said, 'She's with the doctor now.'

Jesse knew how much force was required to knock someone unconscious with a single punch. He told Suit he was on his way.

He used the siren and the flasher.

19

Jesse and Molly and Suit sat in Molly's living room. Jesse and Suit had finally stopped taking turns asking how she was feeling until she finally told them that if they didn't stop she was going to pistol-whip Jesse and then Suit and then Jesse again.

'You're certain the doctor told you that you didn't suffer a concussion?' Jesse said.

'What is this, an interrogation?' she said. 'I already told you he said no. Twice.'

'And you wouldn't lie to a fellow officer of the law about any of this, correct?' Jesse said.

She smiled then. Just like that, she was Molly, if a little worse for wear at the moment, with bruising on one side of her face that was already turning the color of one of her purple orchids.

'A thought like that would never occur to me,' she said.

'You look as if you could use a drink,' Suit said.

'You know something, you're right,' she said. 'Michael's scotch is in the cupboard. Over the drawer where I keep the silverware.'

'I don't know where you keep your silverware,' Suit said.

'You're a detective,' Molly said. 'Figure it out.'

'Make it a double,' Jesse said. 'It'll be like you're having one for me.'

'Wait,' Suit called from the kitchen. 'Is it okay for you to drink if you're taking pain pills?'

'Not taking them,' she called back.

'That's my girl,' Jesse said.

'I can play hurt,' she said. When she smiled this time, she immediately made a face. 'Ow,' she said.

Suit came back with a tumbler filled nearly to the top with scotch. Jesse stared at the color of it and watched his deputy chief take a big swallow, and felt as if he could taste it right along with her.

'Well,' Molly said, 'that hit the spot.'

Every single time, Jesse thought.

All the spots.

He asked her to take him through it again, in case she'd missed something in her first telling.

'I keep thinking I might have missed something,' she said. 'Like you keep going back to The Throw in case *you* might have missed something. It's what we do, right?'

Jesse grinned. 'Well done, grasshopper.'

'Wish I'd known some kung fu today,' Molly said. 'Not that it would have done me much good once they jumped me.'

'Just remember you *did* get jumped,' Jesse said. 'Nothing anybody can do about that.'

Molly said, 'I know I keep coming back to this. Shoot me, I'm a mom. She *does* remind me of my daughters.'

Molly said there was still crime scene tape stripped across the front door when she got there, as Jesse had mandated. But Molly had walked around the house, checking windows, until she got to the back door, which was locked. Then she'd gone back to the front and opened the door with the key she'd picked up at the station.

'I had it in my head that whoever had searched the house might have done the same thing I was doing,' she said.

'Another one of your hunches,' Jesse said.

'Like you always say,' Molly said. 'I can't stop them, I can only hope to contain them.'

She said she'd planned to start in the kitchen, and then work her way across the first floor. She had just walked down the narrow hallway past the stairs that took you to the second floor when she was grabbed from behind, a bear hug so powerful it took the breath out of her.

The second guy pulled her PPD baseball hat down over her eyes, nothing Molly could do to stop him. In the moment, she was trying to breathe as the guy holding her whispered in her ear, 'Did she tell you where it is?'

Molly had managed to squeeze out 'Where *what* is?' at the moment she managed to take a small step forward, create enough space for herself, and kick her right heel into the man's groin.

She heard him cry out in pain, and she had just broken free when she said she walked into the hardest blow to the head she had ever taken in her life, a closed-fist punch she did not see coming, and that put her down and out.

'They had to know we weren't watching the house,' Suit said.

'Because *they* were watching the house,' Jesse said. 'And because Deputy Chief Crane, being a cowboy, had gone there alone.'

'Takes one to know one, cowboy,' Molly said.

She drank more scotch and sighed contentedly. Jesse knew the feeling the way he knew his badge number, the first one and then the next one after that, the warmth beginning to spread like a river running through you, reaching all of your synapses, trying to fill in as many of the junctures between nerve cells as possible.

'Whatever they're looking for must be pretty valuable to somebody,' Suit said.

Jesse looked at Molly and nodded. 'That's the kind of analytical thinking that made *him* a detective.'

'That and being a kiss-up to the chief,' Molly said.

'Takes one to know one,' Suit said to her.

'He wishes,' Molly said to him.

'So somebody, Ben Gage in this case, discovers something that he says could be a game-changer in the land deal, at least according to the message he left for Blair,' Jesse said. 'Maybe he turned up some kind of old easement saying the rights to the land really belong to the town.'

'Easement?' Suit said.

'The chief does more reading than you think,' Molly said.

'Wouldn't Neil have known about something like that?' Suit said.

'Maybe the kid had been doing more than one kind of digging,' Jesse said.

'Whatever it is, it was important enough for these guys to risk going back to the house,' Molly said, 'and assault a police officer.'

'But what?' Suit said.

Jesse shrugged. 'As one of my old watch commanders at Robbery Homicide used to say, there's the rub.'

'Watch Commander Shakespeare?' Molly said.

She was nearly finished with her drink. The first one always went down like that, at least with him.

Even stopping thinking *about drinking was hard.*

'If whatever Ben Gage found was that important, it had to be important to the two guys who want the land,' Molly said. 'And the one trying to sell it.'

'Maybe one guy had the house searched first,' Jesse said, 'and the other guy sent his people over to re-toss the place.'

'Or sent Crow,' Suit said.

In a quiet voice, Molly said, 'Crow wouldn't hit me.'

They sat there in silence then until Suit asked if Molly wanted him to get her another drink. She winked at Jesse and said, 'As a wise man likes to say, I've had enough.'

Jesse said, 'What if Neil O'Hara died because he knew what they were looking for, too?'

'Whatever it is they're looking for,' Molly said.

'You're saying that Ben Gage might have told Neil before he got the chance to tell Blair what it was?' Suit said.

'Maybe by then they really were on the same side,' Jesse said, 'and the kid wanted to share the good news. Or wasn't sure what he had and wanted Neil to look at it.'

'Now it may have gotten him and Blair killed,' Molly said.

'Did Kate mention anything like that?' Suit said.

Jesse shook his head.

'My Irish grandmother used to call a mess like this *praiseach*,' Molly said.

'Showing all signs of being an even worse hairball than I thought,' Jesse said.

He told Suit it was time for him to go home to Elena. He then informed Molly that he'd be sleeping on her couch tonight. Before she could respond he held up a hand and said, 'That's an order.'

'Okay,' she said.

'Finally,' he said.

Molly said, 'You can take one of the girls' rooms.'

'I don't see why they'd take another run at you,' Jesse said. 'But if they do, I'd rather be downstairs when they do.'

'Even with an alarm?' Molly said.

'Ben Gage and Blair Richmond had an alarm, too,' Jesse said.

'What the hell is going on here?' Molly said.

'A good old-fashioned land war,' Jesse said.

20

The next afternoon Jesse was having lunch with Vinnie Morris, who was sitting with his back to the wall – 'What you might call your force a habit,' Vinnie said when he sat down – at a corner table of the Gray Gull, now fully owned by Sunny's friend Spike.

'Your' with Vinnie often came out 'you-ah.'

Vinnie wore a cream-colored suit, a blue shirt the color of a robin's egg, and a silk pocket square the same color as the shirt. If there was a Best-Dressed List for guys in Vinnie's line of work, whatever that was these days, Jesse just assumed Vinnie won it every year. His hair was as dark as it had been since Jesse had first met him. Jesse knew he would never ask if it was the result of genetics or a good colorist, because Vinnie was a much better shot than he was.

Or anyone Jesse had ever known, for that matter.

They both had plates of fried clams in front of them. Vinnie was drinking Coke out of a small bottle. Jesse was having iced tea. Vinnie was a bit behind the news with Jesse and Sunny. Jesse caught him up.

'Idiot,' Vinnie said.

Jesse told him that seemed to be the prevailing theory.

'Fuckin' ay,' Vinnie said.

Vinnie forked a clam, dipped it in his tartar sauce, every moment as precise as a surgeon with a scalpel, as little wasted motion with him as ever, even when chewing.

'Hear Crow is back,' Vinnie said.

'Working for Billy Singer.'

'Heard that, too.'

'You think I need to worry about him?' Jesse said.

'Crow ain't your problem,' Vinnie said. 'He ain't been a problem for you for a long time. Your problem is the other guy.'

'Singer?'

Vinnie shook his head.

'Barrone?' Jesse said.

'Yeah,' Vinnie said.

'Suit asked me before I came over here who I thought was worse,' Jesse said, 'Singer or Barrone.'

Vinnie ate another clam. Now that Jesse thought about it, he wasn't even sure he could tell *if* Vinnie was chewing.

'Spoiler alert?' Vinnie said. 'It ain't close. It's Barrone. Guy's a stone gangster, no offense.'

'None taken.'

'I go back with him to when I was working with Gino,' Vinnie said. 'God rest.'

Gino Fish. Vinnie's old boss. Before him Vinnie had been with Joe Broz, Jesse knew, who'd once been the biggest crime boss in Boston, even bigger than Desmond Burke, Sunny's former father-in-law. It was before Tony Marcus became more powerful than all of them. Jesse had immersed himself in Boston's mob history after he had met Sunny. Sometimes he imagined all of the old bosses having their own baseball cards. Even their own Hall of Fame.

'I know this will sound like an oxymoron,' Jesse said, 'but I was under the impression that Barrone is a legit businessman.'

Vinnie smirked. 'What he wants people to think.'

'Wasn't he going to run for governor once?' Jesse said.

Vinnie made a sound that was as close to laughter as he ever got. 'You mean *that* legit business?' he said.

Also with Vinnie, 'that' occasionally slid into 'dat.'

Vinnie said, 'Put it this way: People who used to cross Ed Barrone on his way up had a way of disappearing. And when somebody would ask him about that, he'd order another round of drinks and say about the guy disappeared, "Did he leave a forwarding address?"'

'Would he kill somebody to get this land?' Jesse said.

'And then kill his dog,' Vinnie said.

Vinnie had finished his lunch. Jesse had barely touched his. They were at the Gull because Vinnie had called him. Vinnie gave a small nod at Jesse's plate now, and Jesse slid it across the table to him.

'Before this is over,' Vinnie said, 'you might be needing Crow to watch your back.'

'Why would I do something like that when I have you?' Jesse said.

'Not right now,' Vinnie said. 'There's a guy from Vegas needs me on a thing. He's made it worth my while. So's I could be there awhile.'

'You hear anything interesting about Billy Singer while you're out there,' Jesse said, 'let me know.'

''Course,' Vinnie said.

'Until then,' Jesse said, 'I can take care of myself.'

'Listen to me on this,' Vinnie said. 'Barrone don't care whether you're a cop or not. Or if Molly is one. He might smile his ass off, he's with you. But he's used to getting what he wants. Or needs. Either way.'

'I will consider myself warned,' Jesse said.

'You know Crow,' Vinnie said. 'What he's capable of, what he's not. What lines he'd cross, which ones he won't. He's like us in the sense that he's got a code. If Barrone ever had a code, he forgot it. Or just doesn't give a shit anymore.'

He pushed his chair back.

'It gets bad here, I can come back,' Vinnie said.

He dropped a fifty-dollar bill that looked as crisp and clean as he was on the table.

'One more thing,' Vinnie said. 'You find out who punched Molly and you can't take care of it, I will.'

'Trust me,' Jesse said, 'if I find out, I won't need anybody else to take care of it.'

'Between two mutts like Singer and Barrone is not anywhere you want to be,' Vinnie said.

Jesse smiled and reminded him that everybody had to be someplace.

'Sure,' Vinnie said.

It came out 'shoo-ah.'

Vinnie walked through the crowded room as easily as a smooth rock skimming across water.

Jesse was in the parking lot when Thomas Lawton called him.

'Get over here,' he said.

'Over where?'

'Where do you think?' Lawton said. 'My graveyard.'

21

Crow knew he should have gone back to check the kids' house the day before; that was just sloppy.

If he had, maybe he could have gotten there before Molly. And before Barrone's guys. Because if they hadn't been Barrone's guys, then whose were they?

Unless of course Billy Singer, who had hired him, had brought in muscle that he hadn't told Crow about. Billy was Vegas, after all, through and through. Maybe Billy Singer, who was who he was, was simply hedging his bets.

Crow was no longer sure why he'd taken this job. He didn't need the money. Unless he got stupid, or careless, or both, he wasn't going to need money ever again, because of what he'd scored off the Jimmy Macklin job. But then he'd come back the first time, after the statute of limitations – ten years – had run out on the stolen money. Then he'd come back again looking for a missing kid, liking the idea of being a tracker again, and because he needed some action. He'd ended up finding the kid, Amber Francisco, and as much of a pain in the ass as she was, he couldn't bring himself to take her back to her father, who in the end only got what he deserved, not the kid.

Now he'd gone to work for Billy Singer. He'd done some work for him a long time ago, when Crow still needed money, even though he didn't have much use for the man. But then Crow had ended up in Vegas a few months ago, shacking up with a dealer he knew from the old days named Bonnie. Or Bunny. Bored again. He didn't care much more for Vegas than he did Billy Singer. But Bonnie or Bunny was working a blackjack table at The House. Crow had run into Billy there one night. Or maybe Billy had seen him on the monitors and run into him.

Now here he was.

Go to Paradise, Billy said, find out who can be bought and who can't, who needs to be persuaded – that's the word Billy used, *persuaded* – to come around to Billy's side on this land deal. Make this easy just so it doesn't get hard.

With a handshake on Crow getting a piece of the deal when it went through.

'We go back, Crow,' Billy said. 'The reason we don't have to write things down is because I know how this goes if I try to screw you on the back end.'

Just like that, Crow was on his way back to Paradise. But was he doing it because he was betting on the come, or because he wanted to see Molly Crane again?

He'd been watching her for a few days before he showed himself to her that night at The Throw. She didn't know he was watching her. No one ever saw Crow if he didn't want them to. He finally *wanted* her to see him that night, even if he knew it would land him in Stone's office. Crow didn't care. It would get him into the room with her, even though Stone would be there, too.

Crow had never felt this way about a woman in his life, even after just one night with her.

One night in Paradise.

Thinking of it that way should have been funny, or dumbassed. Only it wasn't.

For now he sat in his rented car down the street from Kate O'Hara's house on Stiles Island, having bluffed his way past the guy at the gate, wondering how he wanted to play it with her, thinking that maybe she knew more than she said she knew that night before Stone found the body. She'd told him that night that she thought her estranged husband – she called him that every time, stepping on 'estranged' pretty hard – had grown increasingly skeptical that the land deal, even with the money involved, was the best thing for the town. Something about her, though, he liked. Maybe because she was smart. The way Molly was smart.

'It's as if Neil can't see beyond the town line anymore,' Kate told Crow that night he went to her house. 'Or past the Paradise in which he grew up. Then he ended in the middle of all this. And in a lot more pain than he lets on.'

'Was it the land deal causing it?' Crow had said.

She'd given him a long look and finally said, 'Ask him when you catch up with him.'

Crow could tell sometimes when a woman wanted it. Not always. Any man who told you they always knew was full of shit. Did Kate O'Hara want something to happen that night? Did it really matter? Crow wouldn't be around long enough to find out.

He thought Molly still wanted it, though. No matter how much she smart-mouthed him.

He drank coffee out of his thermos and watched the house. Something had brought him here today the way something told him that Kate O'Hara might have been holding back. Maybe if she came out of the house he would follow her. Give him something else to do.

Molly.

He couldn't keep her out of his head for long. He wanted to see her again, he knew that. He didn't like most women, even the ones he'd slept with. He'd always liked her, though, even before they'd ended up together. He liked Stone, too, even though he trusted Jesse Stone about as much as Stone trusted him.

What a place.

There were other cars parked on the street. He was between two of them. Nothing to see for the people walking the street, the mailman, people walking their dogs. Move along.

He had been there about an hour when the black Jag pulled up in front of Kate O'Hara's house.

Then Ed Barrone got out and walked straight to her front door. When Kate O'Hara opened it, he went inside.

22

The corner of The Throw to which Thomas Lawton directed Jesse was at the far northwest corner of the property, where it backed up to the golf club Ed Barrone wanted to expand as part of his vision for this land.

Lawton was staring at Jesse, hands on hips, when Jesse pulled up on the dirt road and got out of his Explorer.

'Took you long enough,' Lawton said.

'What,' Jesse said, 'you didn't hear the siren over the sound of the waves?'

Thomas Lawton was taller than Jesse, clearly a gym rat from the way he was ripped underneath the tight polo shirts he favored. Blond hair cropped close to his head. Rolex watch as big as a baseball.

When Jesse was close enough to him, Lawton pointed at a new headstone and said, 'Look at this shit.'

The headstone was splattered with red paint, but still visible underneath was Lawton's name, his date of birth, and what they both knew was the date when the members of the Board would vote on whether to approve the sale of the land or not. Then they'd open the envelope with the sealed bids inside and announce the winner of the land. Like an awards ceremony.

Or a game show.

For a guy like Lawton, who talked very big and acted just as tough, Jesse thought he might cry.

'I thought you'd hired security,' Jesse said.

'Not twenty-four/seven,' he said.

'Shame,' Jesse said.

'Maybe I ought to put up one of these stones myself,' Lawton said. 'Put that little shit Ben Gage's name on it. And use his real blood.'

'You know he and his girlfriend are missing, right?' Jesse said.

'You want me to feel bad about that, the grief they've caused me?' Lawton said. 'You know what I'd call the loss of a couple of tree huggers? A *start*.'

Jesse knelt down and looked at the letters and the numbers. They looked like all the rest. Same size. Same style with the inscription. Ben Gage and Blair Richmond weren't around. The resistance work went on, clearly.

Jesse looked up at Lawton.

'You always have a lot to say about them,' he said. 'You got any thought on what might have happened to them?'

He stood so they were facing each other. Probably closer than Lawton liked. But he didn't back up.

'Yeah, Stone,' Lawton said. 'I'm this close to hitting the jackpot, but I'm suddenly going to start bumping off people in my way. You can't possibly be looking at me for Neil O'Hara.'

Jesse smiled. 'Should I be?'

'Kiss my ass,' Lawton said.

He walked over to the headstone, maybe as a way of getting out of Jesse's airspace, and pointed to it and said, 'So what are you going to do about this?'

'Treat it like what it is,' Jesse said. 'A threat. Interview all the other members of SOB. Tell them that whoever did this just upped the ante.'

He knew he was lying. It didn't mean Lawton had to know. He was just telling Lawton what he wanted to hear.

'Do these idiots really think they can stop us at this point?' Lawton said. 'The sale is going to go through, and there's nothing they can do about it.'

'How come your father never put the land up for sale?' Jesse said.

'I think he loved this town more than he loved me,' Lawton said. 'But I don't. Love the town, I mean. He made me promise to him, when he was dying, that I'd keep it protected and keep it in the family. I swore I would.' Lawton shrugged. 'But the old man screwed up. He trusted me.'

'You don't have enough money already?' Jesse said.

'Are you drunk?' Lawton said, then grinned and added, 'No offense.'

'None taken,' Jesse said.

'You never have enough,' Lawton said.

'You think selling it is the right thing for the town?'

Lawton barked out a laugh that sounded more than somewhat like a growl to Jesse.

'Little late in the game to start worrying about the rich getting richer in Paradise, wouldn't you say?'

He walked over to the motorbike he'd left leaning against a tree near the road, the one on which Jesse would sometimes see him tooling around town, much too fast.

'And so you know?' Lawton called out to Jesse. 'As soon as the deal is done, I will put this town in my rearview mirror forever.'

Jesse saluted him.

'Who doesn't love a happy ending?' he said to Lawton.

He had gotten back behind the wheel of the Explorer when Crow called and said, 'It's your trusty sidekick.'

Jesse told him he was neither trusty nor a sidekick.

'Figure of speech, *Kemosabe*,' Crow said.

23

They were on a stretch of beach near where Jesse lived. Jesse had brought coffee from Daisy Dyke's. When he ordered two, Daisy had asked who the other was for and Jesse had told her Crow.

Daisy said, 'Let me get him another cup so I can spit in it.'

'He swears he's a law-abiding citizen now,' Jesse had said, 'and friend of the local police.'

'Yeah,' Daisy said, 'and I'm straighter than the Duchess of Cambridge.'

Jesse and Crow sat on a piece of driftwood. When Jesse told him what Daisy Dyke had said, Crow grinned and made a tomahawk chop with his free hand.

'How's Molly feeling?' Crow said.

'You heard.'

'Small town,' Crow said. 'Big mouths.'

'I run into a lot of that,' Jesse said. 'When we find out who hit her, she is quite anxious to get at least one free swing in.'

He sipped some coffee. Crow had poured his into his fancy thermos. Jesse stared out at the water and said, 'You need to stay away from Molly.'

'Be Molly's call on something like that, wouldn't it?'

'Not with me around.'

Crow was staring out at the water himself.

'Always wanted to ask you,' he said. 'If it came down to it, would you have shot me the way you did Jimmy Macklin?'

'If you'd drawn down on me the way he did, sure.'

'I would have known better.'

'So why'd you call?' Jesse said.

'Ed Barrone visited the widow O'Hara a little while ago,' Crow said.

'Really.'

'Really,' Crow said.

'And as a concerned member of the community,' Jesse said, 'you wanted me to know first thing.'

'You were with her once,' Crow said.

Jesse grinned. 'This *is* a small town.'

'You curious about what business Barrone had with the widow?' Crow said.

'You should know by now that my curiosity is practically boundless,' Jesse said.

'I don't know why it would matter to him at this point,' Crow said. 'But maybe she picked a side even though her husband wouldn't. Though once those bids are sealed, I don't see as how it would matter.'

'Maybe they could get unsealed and adjusted before the big reveal,' Jesse said.

'That's a very cynical attitude,' Crow said.

'So shoot me,' Jesse said.

24

Neil O'Hara had bought a small, two-story house between the shopping district and the first houses that were high enough up on Beach Avenue to actually see some of the harbor. Jesse didn't know if Kate had a key to the house, and hadn't asked. Assumed she probably did, but didn't want to wait, so he did what any industrious chief of police would do and picked the lock, just the way Sunny Randall had showed him. One of her many and varied and impressive talents.

Suit and Molly had come here the first morning, telling Jesse afterward that as far as they could tell, after a thorough search, that things looked to them the way Neil must have left them the last time he was in the house. They had taken Neil's laptop with them and turned it over to Gabe Weathers, the best techy in the department, but he said there was nothing in the browsing history that looked to him like a smoking gun. So to speak, Gabe had said. He was still working on what he called cloud extraction, which he said was about as easy as learning how to build a rocket from scratch without a password.

Jesse stood in the small den in the back of the house now, the one that Neil had used as a home office. There was a decent view of the harbor through the bay window back here.

What had Neil been thinking about the last time he'd looked out this window?

There wasn't much bare space on the walls. Law diploma. A posed shot of Neil with the other members of the current Board of Selectmen. Team photos from his high school baseball team, year by varsity year. There was a series of photographs, black-and-white, of Neil's father with his crew from the B-24 Liberators in which his dad, Jesse knew, had been a bombardier during World War II. And one of Neil's grandfather, who'd himself been police chief in Paradise once.

Mostly there was baseball stuff in the office. A lot of it. An old photograph of Babe Ruth in a Red Sox uniform. A signed Ted Williams poster that somebody had given him. A similar poster, just as big, framed, of David Ortiz. A *Boston Globe* front page from 2004, when the Red Sox won a World Series that felt like their first since tribes had roamed the land. A much bigger display of signed baseballs under glass. A drawing of the original Fenway Park. Photographs from the day he'd been signed in as mayor. An ancient-looking black-and-white photograph of an Indian chief. Or should Jesse think of him as Native American, even though he was probably called an Indian in the old days? A photograph of Neil's parents' wedding. A replica of the Town Charter.

Just stuff. But stuff that mattered to Neil. Jesse felt as if he were taking a brief tour through the man's history. Which also had mattered in Paradise, Mass.

Jesse went through the drawers now, and the one floor-to-ceiling bookcase. Looked underneath the desk for some kind of hidden compartment. He lifted a little stone bowl being used as a paperweight for the printout record of the last Board meeting over which he'd presided.

Then Jesse went through the rest of the house as if going through it for the first time. Room by room. Cupboard by cupboard in the kitchen. The closet and the drawers and the bedside table in the bedroom. What was he looking for?

Something. Anything that would help him understand how his friend had been the one to end up in one of those shallow graves.

But came up with nothing. It bothered him that he couldn't find a cell phone, not in the house, not in the old Chevy parked in the garage. The car had been here the night he died, they'd checked. It meant someone had taken Neil to The Throw, either dead or alive. *Curiouser and curiouser.* Which character in *Alice's Adventures in Wonderland* had said that? Jesse was pretty sure it had been Alice. Molly would know. Sunny would know. Crow had asked if Jesse was curious about Kate knowing Ed Barrone. Normally that would have been her business, except when it intersected with Jesse's.

He knew this: If Ben Gage and Neil O'Hara had been seen as a threat, so, too, was Jesse now. Small town, Crow kept saying. Small enough for all involved parties to know Jesse's history, that he would eventually find out who had done it, and why.

He went back to the study one last time, stood in the middle of the room, and said, 'Talk to me.'

Nothing in there did.

He wondered again if someone had searched this place the night Neil died, just not tossing it the way Ben and Blair's house had been tossed. Or maybe it was different people doing the searching. Another possibility. Maybe, Jesse thought, he should put a car out front, all day every day in the short run, on the chance they might come back. Whoever they were. Whatever they were looking for. But knew he didn't have the manpower for that. So he went back to the Explorer now and got the motion sensor out of the glove compartment and came back and set it in the front room. Cost him twenty bucks on Amazon. He'd been waiting to use it. *CSI Paradise,* he thought.

He made his way back home eventually, fried himself some chicken sausage and potatoes, fell asleep in front of another Red Sox game, went to bed for good around eleven o'clock, and slept until Molly called him a little before five in the morning to tell him that they'd found Ben Gage's body in some woods over near the Marshport ravine.

25

The body was already gone by the time Jesse got there. He still wanted to see where a couple hikers had discovered the grave somebody had dug, covering it with dirt and branches. Knowing it would be discovered eventually, but perhaps not for a while.

Another grave, Jesse thought, *this time with the kid who'd been digging them in Paradise in it.*

He was standing with Brian Lundquist's number two in the Homicide division of the state cops, an ex-UMass tight end named Booker Mays.

'He still had his wallet on him,' Mays said. 'When I told Lundquist who it was, he said I should call you.'

'He's a big fan of mine,' Jesse said.

'Not sure I'd put it that way,' Mays said. 'But he's been following what you got going on over there in your town.'

'All of which just got worse,' Jesse said.

'We called in one of our examiners,' Mays said. 'She said she couldn't be sure, but it looked like the kid had been dead a couple of days.'

Mays turned and spit some tobacco.

'He looked like he got beat up pretty bad,' he said. 'Before they put one through the back of his head.'

Jesse said, 'Where's your boss, by the way?'

'Hangin' out down there in Beacon Hill with the fancy people,' he said.

Sunny's neighborhood.

Not everybody was fancy down there.

'Somebody shot a judge,' Mays said. 'In bed with another judge's wife.'

'Couldn't keep it in his robe,' Jesse said.

'Flesh is weak,' Mays said.

'The kid had gone missing around the time somebody shot our mayor,' Jesse said.

'Missing on his own?'

'Or on the run,' Jesse said. 'Until he got caught.'

'You want to talk about it?' Mays said.

'Long story,' Jesse said.

'I rarely run into any short ones,' Booker Mays said.

Jesse kept staring down at the shallow grave. He had never met Ben Gage. Now he was dead, most likely over dirt he and Blair Richmond and their friends thought was worth fighting for, even though they weren't in it for the money.

Jesse decided he might pop the next person he heard call them tree huggers.

At least he knew where Ben Gage was now.

Where was Blair Richmond?

'This all over that land deal?' Mays said.

'There are people in my town who thought this kid was standing in the way of a big score for some powerful people, and all the people in town who could make smaller scores.'

'Land worth killing over?' Mays said.

'Gonna find out,' Jesse said. 'Or die trying.'

Mays grinned. 'How come with you,' he said, 'that doesn't sound like a figure of speech?'

Jesse walked out of the woods then. Maybe there could possibly have been a lousier way to start his day. He couldn't think of one, offhand.

26

Ed Barrone didn't like being summoned to Jesse's office, and had delivered a rather lengthy soliloquy on that subject as soon as he'd shown up, even after being told what had happened to Ben Gage.

When he finally finished, Jesse calmly told him he wasn't as interested as Barrone might think about what he did and didn't like now that he had another dead body on his hands.

Then he walked around to Barrone's side of his desk, swiveled his laptop so it was facing Barrone, and hit play, and then they both listened to Barrone tell the town's ace reporter, Nellie Shofner, on her podcast that in his day, these damn tree huggers would have been taken for a ride.

There was more. But that was the money quote. Jesse sat back down in his chair and crossed his arms.

'I was just kidding around,' Barrone said.

Jesse nodded. 'What they all say.'

'They've been busting our balls,' he said. 'I decided to bust theirs a little.'

'*Our* balls?' Jesse said. 'I had no idea you were that much of a team player.'

'Mine, Lawton's, even that hump Singer's,' Barrone said. 'Like it or not, we're all in this together.'

Ed Barrone, Jesse knew, had been a boxer as a kid. Heavyweight. He could see it in the scar tissue around his eyes, and a nose that seemed flatter than it once had been. But he looked as if he still kept himself in shape. There was a lot of steel-gray hair, brushed straight back from his forehead. Big hands. A loud voice. He seemed to take up more space than just his own, and most of the oxygen in the room.

'What, you think I had something to do with that kid getting shot?' Barrone said. 'This close to getting what I want? In what world?'

'Lawton said the same thing,' Jesse said. 'Doesn't mean things can't change on the ground, especially if the whole deal somehow starts to look like less of a sure thing.'

'Nobody could stop it even if they wanted to,' Barrone said.

'Ben Gage still seemed to think he could.'

'How?'

'For me to find out,' Jesse said.

Then he told him about Ben Gage's message to Blair Richmond before she'd disappeared.

'I don't know anything about that,' Barrone said. 'Maybe he had something on Singer. Found out where *his* bodies were buried. Maybe he caught Singer in some kind of bribe. Who the fuck knows.'

'But nothing on you,' Jesse said.

'Not a chance in hell,' Barrone said.

'Because of a life of good works,' Jesse said.

'I didn't say that,' Barrone said.

'You've made a lot of enemies,' Jesse said.

'Because I don't lose,' he said. 'Okay? I do not lose. The guy who should be sitting across from you is Singer. I just want this deal to go through. But I hear he needs it to go through. You spin plates as long as he has, eventually they all come crashing down.'

'Funny,' Jesse said. 'Singer says you're the one who needs this deal.'

'He said that about me?' Barrone said. 'What a piece of shit.'

'Nevertheless.'

Barrone leaned forward so his elbows were on Jesse's desk, chin on his big hands.

'Where do you weigh in on this deal, Chief?' he said.

'I just want what's best for the town,' Jesse said.

'Then you should be backing me,' Barrone said. 'Me getting the land is best for the town, not some spray-tan phony from Vegas.'

'You ever meet the kid Gage?'

'No,' Barrone said.

'What about Blair Richmond?'

'Who's she?'

'I didn't say it was a woman,' Jesse said. 'Blair could be a guy's name.'

'Don't start that shit,' Barrone said.

'She was Ben Gage's girlfriend,' Jesse said. 'Now she's disappeared.'

'I know nothing about anything like that.'

'A guy I trust told me that when you were on your way up in the construction business,' Jesse said, 'guys who crossed you used to disappear from time to time.'

'I'm telling you,' Barrone said, 'you're confusing me with the other guy.'

He smiled. His teeth weren't nearly as white as Billy Singer's.

'Are *you* done busting balls now?' he said to Jesse. 'Because if you are, I'm a busy guy.'

'Not too busy to visit Kate O'Hara,' Jesse said.

Barrone colored slightly. And something changed in his eyes. Like the old fighter had been hit.

But he rallied.

'You got a tail on me?' he said.

'Heard it from a friend of a friend,' Jesse said.

Barrone stood up now. But the smile was back in place.

'People told me not to underestimate you,' Ed Barrone said.

'Aw, shucks,' Jesse said.

27

Spike was at the Gray Gull tonight. Jesse was meeting Kate O'Hara and arrived early.

'Should I even ask about how things are going with our friend in L.A.?' Spike said.

'No,' Jesse said.

Spike said, 'Hard no?'

'Really hard,' Jesse said.

Spike pointed to the corner table in the front room and said, 'Do you mind if I give you the table in which you and the person we're not talking about who's in L.A. right now used to sit?'

'Knock yourself out.'

'Dinner for two often means a date,' Spike said.

'This is work,' Jesse said.

He saw Spike's eyebrows raise suddenly, and saw that Kate was coming through the door.

'All work and no play,' Spike said.

'I could knock *you* out,' Jesse said.

'Right this way, Chief Stone,' Spike said brightly.

Kate wasn't as beautiful as Sunny was. No woman Jesse had ever been with was as beautiful as Sunny, not even Jenn. Kate had still looked beautiful to Jesse even when he had gone to the house before dawn that morning. But tonight was different. She was still the widow O'Hara, and had even worn a simple black dress. No jewelry except, Jesse noticed, her wedding ring. Very little makeup, but then she'd rarely worn a lot of makeup. He liked her hair short. But he had always liked everything about her. As they took their seats Jesse remembered other nights at the Gull for the two of them, before Spike owned it. Before Sunny. He wasn't sure if it was always this table. Sometimes it was. Maybe Kate didn't feel the old connections he was feeling.

She was married to your friend.

'I assume this is business and not pleasure,' she said.

'It's still a pleasure to be across the table from you,' Jesse said. 'Even if things have changed between us.'

'A lot of things,' she said.

It was not a night for small talk, and they both knew it, even though each made a half-hearted attempt. She said that she was planning a memorial service for Neil once they got past the vote. She asked if Jesse had made progress on his investigation of Neil's death. He said some. She asked about Ben Gage's death. He told her that he'd been beaten and then shot, nobody trying to make it look like a suicide with him.

'The way you think they did with Neil?' she said.

He said, 'Whoever tried with Neil was just sloppy enough.'

'You think that boy's death is related to Neil's,' she said.

'I do,' he said. 'I think both of them were standing in the way of progress. And now they aren't.'

He drank some of his iced tea. She had barely touched her white wine.

'They knew something that they weren't supposed to know,' he said. 'Or had something they weren't supposed to have.'

'But what?'

'Don't know,' he said, and then added, 'yet.'

She smiled. He had always thought her smile made her even lovelier. Younger, even. It was a good damned smile regardless.

'A lot of things *have* changed,' she said. 'But you haven't.'

'Well,' he said, 'I haven't had a drink today.'

'You weren't so bad when you were drinking,' she said.

'Actually,' he said, 'I was worse.'

She took a sip of her wine now. He knew he was as attracted to her, right here and right now, as he had ever been. Drunk or sober. But he *had* been drunk a lot of the time when they were together. He wished he remembered more about the time when he thought the two of them had it right, and might even have had a chance. One more thing lost in the fog of boozing, and regrets.

They were waiting for their entrées. Kate had ordered the catch of the day. He'd already forgotten what it was. He'd ordered a burger.

'Got a couple of things I hoped you might clear up for me,' Jesse said.

'Okay.'

'How come you didn't tell me that Wilson Cromartie stopped by your house the night I found Neil?'

'The Native American man?' she said.

'Him.'

'He'd called and said he was representing Billy Singer, and asked if he could come by and ask a few questions,' Kate said. 'He said he was having some difficulty locating Neil, and asked if I might know where he was. I told him that Neil had asked me to have dinner, and that was the last I'd heard from him, and reminded him that Neil and I had been estranged for some time. Then Mr Cromartie got a phone call and left.'

'That was it?'

'What more could there possibly be?' she said. 'People still must have assumed I had more influence with Neil than I did.'

'Like Ed Barrone?' Jesse said.

'What about Ed Barrone?'

'He paid you a visit as well.'

She had just put down her wineglass but picked it back up, as if it were a prop and she needed to do something with her hand.

'Where did *that* come from?' she said.

'A restless mind?'

The waiter brought them their food. When he left she said, 'He came to pay his respects.'

'Took him long enough.'

'Even though Neil is gone,' she said, 'he still has a lot going on.'

'Don't we all,' Jesse said.

'Might I ask you how you know he was at the house?'

'Small town,' he said.

Never failed. Sometimes Jesse thought playing the small-town card could stop beach erosion.

'Were you having me watched, Jesse?' she said.

'Ed asked me the same question,' he said.

'Is that an answer?'

He smiled, trying to defuse the sudden tension between them.

'I'm the chief of police,' he said. 'I get to ask the questions. But the answer is no, Kate. I am not having you watched.'

She stared down at her food, as if she'd forgotten that it was still here.

'He's an old friend,' she said. 'We met in Boston a hundred or so years ago. I hadn't seen him since then until he came to Paradise. He seemed hopeful I might be able to help him with the Board, because we'd known each other. I disavowed him of the notion.'

'Were the two of you ever involved?'

'God, no.'

'Had to ask.'

'Did you really?'

She stared at him until she took her napkin off her lap and placed it next to her plate.

'I seem to have lost my appetite,' she said. 'But being interrogated by an old friend will do that to a girl.'

'Not my intent, Kate,' he said.

She started to push back her chair.

'I think I'd like to leave now,' she said.

'I'll walk you to your car,' Jesse said.

'Not necessary.'

'I insist.'

'Who am I to argue with the chief?' she said.

Kate went to the ladies' room, came back out, said good night to Spike as they passed him. Jesse handed Spike his credit card and said he'd be right back. Spike looked past him at their table and said, 'You don't eat, you don't pay.'

'What about the drinks?'

'On me,' Spike said.

There was one last awkward moment when Jesse and Kate stood next to her two-seater BMW, one she'd had since they'd been dating. Even the way he'd blown up the evening, he was suddenly aware of the closeness of her, the scent of her. Her whole impressive self.

'I'm sorry,' he said.

'So am I,' Kate said.

Then she reached over and put a cool hand to the side of his face and kissed him softly before getting into her car and driving away.

He was a block away from the Gull when he heard a ping from his phone and saw that it was from the motion detector he'd left just inside the front door of Neil O'Hara's house.

28

Jesse knew he should call for backup, knew that if a situation developed at the house he would hear it from Molly tomorrow. But it might be a false alarm. The gadget had cost him only twenty dollars and he'd used it only one other time. If it wasn't a false alarm, he wanted to control the situation himself, and not spook whoever was inside.

And he was only a couple blocks away.

If it was a simple B&E, he would arrest them and take them in. If it was someone who had come to search Neil's house – or had come back to search it again – Jesse wanted to know who it was.

Right fucking now.

He parked at the head of the street and jogged the rest of the way to the house. No lights inside, but that meant nothing; Jesse remembered the shades and draperies being drawn when he was the one who had broken into the place.

He hadn't locked the front door behind him after he'd picked the lock. He was hoping that if someone was still inside, they hadn't, either.

Unless they'd come through the back door and not activated the sensor until they got near the front entrance.

Back or front?

Jesse decided on front.

He had his Glock out, hanging at his side, not pressed to his chest the way he'd been taught for situations involving pursuit. Only this wasn't pursuit, at least not yet. He heard his own breathing as he crouched down and crabbed his way across the front of the house, getting even lower as he passed underneath the picture window in the living room. Down the street and down the hill, he could hear the ocean. It seemed to him that no matter where he was in Paradise, he could hear the ocean. Sometimes he imagined hearing it when he was behind his desk. He gave a last check of his phone, having already muted it, knowing that an incoming call right now would sound like a grenade going off.

The sensor was still activated. Someone was still inside. No light from in there, no sound. Why had he left the sensor?

He knew. Molly wasn't the only one who had hunches.

He put his gun in his left hand and reached up with his right and gently put it on the knob and moved it maybe a quarter of a turn to the right. It moved noiselessly.

He had the element of surprise on his side.

But not much use if he was outnumbered, and outgunned.

There was no one on the street at this time of night. No cars had driven by since Jesse had gotten out of the Explorer. Just the faint light of the moon working its way through the cloud cover. He reached down again, made sure the radio on his belt was disabled.

He turned the knob all the way and pushed the door open and stepped into the front hall. As he did he saw a figure step out into the other end of the hall, just outside the doorway leading to Neil O'Hara's study.

'Police!' Jesse yelled.

He couldn't see whether the man had a gun in his hand or

not. But it didn't matter because the guy turned and bolted for the back of the house, where Jesse knew the kitchen door opened onto the backyard.

Then someone was throwing a shoulder into Jesse from his left, out of the living room, knocking him down, heading for the back door himself, the guy turning and firing a wild shot over Jesse's head that splintered the front door.

Jesse scrambled back to his feet and chased them through the open door, pulling the radio off his belt as he did, yelling that shots had been fired on Beach Avenue and that he was in pursuit of multiple suspects.

As he got to the patio he saw them to his right, cutting across a neighbor's lawn, heading back for the street and probably the beach. They had a good head start. There was enough light from the moon for Jesse to see that they were both dressed in dark clothes. Jesse ran hard after them, readying to drop and roll if one of them stopped and turned and took dead aim at him this time.

He could see them sprinting toward the place where the street dead-ended at the public beach. He knew this area. He often walked it in the night, and wondered if they knew about the wooded area down to their right.

They ran right, toward the woods.

But Jesse was gaining ground.

He saw one of them slowing down now, checking to see where Jesse was, and when he did there was enough light from the moon that Jesse could see it reflecting off what looked like a long handgun.

He heard the first siren in the distance, from the direction of town. The backup he knew he should have called for in the first place.

The man fired the gun and missed him. Jesse dropped to the sand and was about to fire back when he saw the couple walking hand in hand down near the water.

It was then that he heard one shot, and then another, and

then another from behind him, like thunderclaps, as the men on the beach disappeared into the woods.

Jesse rolled over in the sand then and saw Crow standing next to the DEAD END sign, gun in his hand.

29

A half-hour later, Jesse and Crow and Molly and Suit were still sitting on Neil O'Hara's front steps. Jesse wanted to tell Molly that the look she was giving him didn't scare him nearly as much as it used to, but she would have known he was lying.

'Gee, it's like an old Western,' Molly said in the voice Suit said had special sauce to it, nodding at Jesse and Crow. 'Cowboy and Indian.'

'That is what is known as an outdated cultural reference,' Jesse said.

'You're welcome,' Crow said to Molly.

'For what?' she said.

Putting the look on Crow now, who seemed spectacularly unaffected by it.

'For saving Chief Jesse from maybe getting himself shot up good tonight,' Crow said.

'Chief Jesse,' Jesse said. 'Now he makes me sound like the Indian.'

'This isn't funny,' Molly said. 'You *could* have gotten shot.'

'Saved by my trusty companion,' Jesse said.

'Getting less funny as you go,' she said.

'You didn't ask me, boss, but I'd quit while I was behind,' Suit said.

Crow said he had been cruising the town, the way he did most nights, mostly out of boredom. Wondering all over again what he was doing here, no matter what Billy Singer had promised him on the back end. He told them it had taken him only one night to figure out a way to get on the PPD radio frequency. So he had heard Jesse's call for backup. Had been only a few blocks away. Told Jesse he figured he could beat the cavalry.

Or be the cavalry.

Everybody was using Old West references tonight, like once you started you couldn't stop.

'Looked to me like he had you lined up,' Crow said to Jesse. 'He didn't expect somebody to be covering you from the road.'

'But you didn't put him down,' Jesse said.

'Wasn't trying to,' Crow said. 'And that couple was in my line of fire, too.'

Suit and Gabe had already been inside the house, dusting it for prints, when Jesse and Crow had walked back up Beach Ave. Jesse said he would do a walk-through to see if he could tell if anything was missing from his last visit.

'Who do you think they were?' Jesse said to Crow.

'Had to be the same ones who jumped Molly.'

'Looking for what they didn't find at Ben Gage's house,' Jesse said.

He turned on the bottom step so he was facing Crow, dressed in black as usual, like he was trying to blend in with the rest of the night.

'Billy ever mention to you that the kid Gage might have something that threatened the deal?' Jesse said.

Crow shook his head.

'You sure?' Jesse said.

'I'm on your side, remember?' Crow said.

'You're on your side,' Molly said, 'like always.'

Crow stared at her until she turned her attention back to Jesse.

'If you had called for backup we could have covered the back of the house,' she said.

'I'm working on delegating more,' Jesse said.

'Work harder,' she said.

99

She stood up. Jesse took a closer look at her. Middle of the night, early in the morning, it didn't matter. There was always something fresh about her, and not just her mouth. As if she couldn't be anything other than Molly. But as well as Jesse knew her, as close as they were, he knew there were always going to be parts of herself, or places, that the rest of the world couldn't reach.

Like the part of her that knew whether or not she still had feelings for Crow.

'See you at the office,' she said to Jesse.

To Crow she simply said, 'Wilson.'

'Molly.'

'Blair Richmond is still out there somewhere,' she said.

'We hope,' Suit said.

'More faith than hope,' Molly, the good Catholic girl, said. 'Believing what we can't see.'

'Amen,' Jesse said.

'Shut it,' she said, and glared at him one last time, and left.

30

Crow knew that as small as Paradise really was, somehow Barrone had managed to keep a low enough profile even with all the high-profile shit going on around him.

Only now here was Barrone, big as life, the night after the shots had been fired at Neil O'Hara's, having dinner at the Gray Gull with one of the two women from the town's Board Crow had talked to. Morton? Morris? Crow couldn't remember for sure, and who gave a shit, anyway? Clearly Barrone was like a politician, still grinding away to the end.

Crow had come into the Gull for a drink, bored out of his ass again, another night in Paradise stretching out ahead of him like whatever road he'd finally take out of town.

He was drinking Johnnie Walker Blue these days because he could afford it, wondering the same thing he wondered every night he was still in this goddamn town: What was Molly Crane doing right now? He knew her husband was still out there on the ocean somewhere, not sure when he would be coming back. But not back yet. Crow thought about taking a drive past her house, but what good would that do him if he didn't stop? And he'd promised Stone he'd stay away from her.

He couldn't help himself. He *did* like Stone, even knowing if he ever got sideways with him how hard Jesse Stone would come at him. He didn't know for sure if he'd actually saved Stone's life the other night. If he had, Crow felt good about that. About saving a cop's life. Who knew?

Maybe that turned out to be his real work here, not being some kind of glorified advance man for Billy Singer. But he hadn't come here thinking people would die over this piece of land, no matter how valuable it was. But now two were dead and a nice kid, the girl, was missing.

He drank some Blue Label. He knew by now how much easier it went down than the cheaper stuff.

He knew why Singer and Barrone were in it. They were both pigs and their blood feud had been going on for a long time, and the thought of losing to the other guy put their balls in a wringer. And he knew why Lawton, the rich boy who owned the land, was in it. Because he was as much a pig as either Billy Singer or Ed Barrone, and wanted to get paid.

But which one of these bastards would kill to get what they wanted?

And what did they think Neil O'Hara and the tree hugger had that scared the living shit out of all of them?

'Fuckety fuck,' he said.

A Stone expression.

'Excuse me, sir?' the bartender said.

'Talking to myself,' Crow said.

He was deciding whether to have another drink when he saw Barrone calling for his check. Did he have something going with the lady from the Board? She seemed to have some miles on her, but wasn't bad-looking. Decent figure, he remembered from the time he'd talked to her.

Crow watched Barrone get up now, go around the table, pull out the Board lady's chair for her, and he ducked his head until they were out the door. Her car was across the lot. She walked to it now. Barrone had used the valet, handed his ticket to the parking kid, checked his phone while he waited, then put it to his ear and started talking. Crow had given the parking kid twenty bucks. If his rental were any closer to the front door, it would have been parked next to the host stand. Barrone's Jag, the sweet ride he'd seen at Kate O'Hara's house, came around. He got in. Crow had kept the keys to the rental after he'd tipped the kid. He left the restaurant, got behind the wheel now, and followed Barrone, for no other reason than he was *still* bored out of his ass.

Crow managed to stay far enough behind the Jag as it made its way through the downtown area, making a turn at the top of Beach Ave. He knew from Billy Singer that the house Barrone had rented was over near the harbor. But he wasn't heading that way, making a couple more turns and then over the bridge to Stiles Island.

Crow knew his way around now, had taken this route plenty of times since he'd been back in Paradise. Suddenly realized where Barrone was going now, even if he couldn't believe it.

Billy Singer's house.

31

It was one of those nights when Jesse couldn't sleep. Just happened that way sometimes, no way for him to anticipate it, not after all the nights when he'd fallen asleep in front of ballgames and sometimes didn't awaken until three in the morning.

Different from the times when he'd pass out drunk on the same couch. When he wasn't waking up so much as coming to.

Just not tonight. Another day sober. Day at a time. Intellectually, Jesse knew the program worked. But there were times when he wanted to take out his Glock and shoot what they called the Big Book in AA and all the slogans in it full of holes.

'I got sick and tired of being sick and tired.' You heard that one all the time. Sometimes, not that Jesse would ever admit it to Dix or at a meeting, the thing that made him feel that way was people *talking* about being sick and tired.

Maybe he was just tired, even if that meant too tired for sleep. The shit you thought about late at night.

'Let go and let God.' That was another one. But how had God helped Neil O'Hara? Or Ben Gage, who thought he was helping save the world by saving Paradise from developers?

How was God helping Blair Richmond, who was hiding or – more likely – as dead as her boyfriend?

Molly, the good Catholic girl, liked to say that God delivering you from evil was only Her part-time job, as far as she could tell.

Jesse wanted to run it all past Sunny. That's what he'd always done when he was working on a new case, what she'd done when she was working on a case of her own. He'd call her when he was jammed. She'd call him. Often at this time of the night. They'd start talking, start kicking ideas and theories and possible clues and theories around, and suddenly, out of nowhere, it would be as if one of them had found the light switch in a darkened room.

Or a way out of a locked one.

But he knew he wasn't calling her tonight. Or anytime soon. He had no way of knowing if she was back with Tony Gault just because he was now a client of hers. But he had this feeling she might be. There had been only two relationships of note for her since she and her ex-husband had broken up, apart from the times when she and her ex-husband would get back together. There had been Jesse, and there had been Tony Gault. She'd always described Gault as a Hollywood phony when his name came up. Or was 'Hollywood phony' redundant? She'd hooked up with him anyway.

At least the Hollywood phony hadn't tried to drink himself out of his career the way Jesse had, insofar as Jesse knew. Maybe bullshitting people was his drug of choice.

Had nothing to do with where they all were now, whether Sunny was sleeping with Gault again or not. She was a grown-up, as smart about things as Molly was, the way women always seemed to be smarter about things then men, at least in Jesse's view of the world.

But as smart as Molly was, she'd ended up in bed with Crow.

Goddamn, he was tired.

He had spent the day recanvassing the other four members of the Board of Selectmen who weren't Gary Armistead, asking them all, all over again, if they had been pressured by either side on the land deal. Or had been offered bribes. He knew they'd all talked to Crow. He knew they'd all talked to Barrone's lawyer, a headbanger named Steve LaMonica whom Barrone had grown up with in South Boston. A few of them talked about how Gary Armistead, now that he was mayor, sometimes acted as if he wanted the deal to be consummated more than Thomas Lawton did.

This afternoon Jeannie Morton, the longest-serving member of the Board and someone Jesse had briefly dated after first arriving in Paradise, had said to Jesse, 'Gary acts like it's his land, and not Thomas Lawton's.'

'Invested, is he?' Jesse had said.

'Like the rest of us are invested in oxygen,' Jeannie said.

'Care to tell me which way you're going to vote?' Jesse said.

'A girl still needs her secrets,' she said.

'Barrone took you to dinner,' Jesse said.

Jeannie winked at him. 'Not a secret when it's dinner for two at the Gull,' she said. 'And, let's face it, Jesse, a night out at the Gull is way too small to be a bribe.'

Molly had been making another deep digital dive looking for any possible leads or clues about where Blair Richmond might be. Without success. Still no presence for her, for a couple weeks, on TikTok or Instagram. No cash withdrawals from the bank account she'd shared with Ben Gage. No credit card charges since a diner in Marshport the day before she'd dropped out of sight, and seemingly off the edge of the planet. Maybe both of them had stashed emergency money somewhere, if they had to leave Paradise in a hurry, as if they both thought they were in some kind of spy movie.

Suit had told Jesse that Neil's cell phone records were going to be hard to get, because the phone he used had been given to him by the town and was officially public property. Normally on a homicide, the district attorney would fast-track records like these. But when Jesse had asked Ellis Munroe to subpoena Neil's records, he'd said that the only person who was treating Neil's death as a homicide was Jesse, and that he needed more than him being a left-handed thrower and the angle of the bullet being curious to go to a judge. And told him to come back if, and when, he did have more. Jesse was sure Munroe was just busting balls here, but was also sure he could do nothing about it. Jesse knew how the game had changed during the pandemic, and how many criminal cases got shot down. Munroe made it clear that he wasn't going to risk Jesse making a rush to judgment on a case for homicide that would eventually get kicked to the curb.

'There's a new sheriff in town,' Munroe had told him. 'And it's not you, Chief.'

There had been no activity, Suit said, on Blair's phone number since she'd disappeared.

'She's alive,' Molly had just told Jesse on the phone.

'Because you want to believe that?'

'Because I can't not believe it,' Molly said.

Jesse was at the kitchen table now, having moved from room to room. Restless like that. He knew a cup of coffee was a particularly dumb idea for a guy as smart as the chief of police liked to think that he was.

But any kind of stimulant had always been a dumb idea for Jesse, *particularly* at this time of night.

He didn't get out his yellow legal pad, the way he usually did when he was trying to organize his thoughts. He got out a stack of different-colored index cards, feeling a little anal about doing it, and started writing down names and events, trying to establish a useful timeline, one he could actually see on the table in front of him, not on some computer screen.

He moved a few of the cards around a bit. At the top of them was Neil O'Hara's napkin, with <u>NEVER</u> written on it.

One piece of valuable property. Two men wanting it. Badly. Two people dead. Maybe three. Most of the town wanting the deal to go through, thinking that once again the streets of Paradise would be paved with gold.

But not everybody in town.

Certainly not the kids from Save Our Beach.

Then he was done, at least for tonight. Past one in the morning by now. Still only ten o'clock or so on Sunny Standard Time in Southern California. He reached for his phone. Put it right back down, telling himself that the next time they spoke she would be the one to call him.

What is this, high school?

He thought he might be ready to try to sleep again when his phone rang and he saw that it was Molly calling.

'Maybe shots fired at the house Billy Singer is renting,' she said, and then gave Jesse the address and told him she'd meet him there.

'If you beat me there, wait,' Jesse said.

'Yeah,' Molly said. 'Like you always wait for me.'

32

Molly was waiting for Jesse out front. Her Cherokee was parked next to another car. Jesse told her that the other car looked an awful lot like Crow's rental.

'Only because it is,' she said.

Jesse said, 'And what good could possibly come of that?'

'Wilson may be under the impression that he is now deputized because he rode to the rescue the other night,' Molly said.

'I was hoping it was more an implied type thing,' Jesse said.

'The neighbor who called it in wasn't sure it was even gunshots, because Billy's house is set so far back from the road,' she said.

'"Gunshots" plural?' Jesse said.

'So she said.'

'Any activity from inside since you got here?' Jesse said.

'I was only a couple minutes ahead of you,' she said. 'But no.'

Jesse grinned and nodded at the big house at the top of the hill, outlined against the night sky.

'Shall we?' he said.

They walked up the long driveway. The garage doors were shut. Only one car. A black Jaguar.

'Billy Singer been riding around town in a Jag?' Jesse said.

'Didn't he tell you he had a driver?' Molly said.

'I believe he did,' Jesse said, 'now that I think of it.'

'So we've got at least two visitors,' Molly said. 'Your friend Wilson Cromartie and the driver of the Jag. You want me to call the desk and have them run the plates? They're Massachusetts.'

'How about we let them surprise us,' Jesse said, 'after we surprise them?'

The front door was unlocked. Jesse and Molly walked in, guns in hand, Jesse calling out, 'Paradise police.'

'In here.'

Crow.

They followed the sound of his voice through a large foyer and into a much larger living room.

And there they all were.

'Let's get this party started,' Crow said.

Jesse said, 'Looks as if it already has.'

33

Billy Singer was seated on one couch. Ed Barrone was across from him on the other.

Two other guys were seated on the floor in front of the fireplace. White guys, dark clothes. Like they'd been raised to be perps. Both with that sullen perp stare Jesse had been looking at his whole cop life.

As soon as Jesse and Molly had stepped into the room, Singer and Barrone began trying to outshout and outcurse each other, before Jesse snapped at them to both shut the fuck up.

'You can't talk to me that way,' Singer and Barrone said, almost in the same moment.

'Just did,' Jesse said.

In a much quieter voice Crow said, 'I felt threatened by the two desperados on the floor.'

'Explains why you were forced to draw your weapon,' Jesse said.

'Practically feared for my life, not ashamed to say,' Crow said.

The guy on the floor without the hat said, 'Bull. Shit.'

Jesse ignored him.

'Who brought you two boys to the dance?' Jesse said to the two in front of the fireplace.

'They work for me,' Singer said.

Jesse said to Crow, 'You ever meet them before?'

'Not till now,' Crow said.

'You need more muscle than Crow?' Jesse said to Billy Singer. 'Seriously? What, the Navy SEALs were busy?'

'Needs more muscle now,' Crow said. 'I just put in my papers.'

'Fuck off, Crow,' Singer said, and Crow put eyes on him until Singer turned away.

Barrone got up off the couch.

'I'm out of here,' he said.

'Sit down,' Jesse said, with enough snap in his voice that Ed Barrone hesitated just briefly before doing just that.

'I assume your friends over there are no longer armed,' Jesse said to Crow.

'Not now they're not,' he said, and pointed with his own gun at the two Beretta long guns at his feet.

'Who fired the shots?' Molly said.

'I did when they wouldn't behave,' Crow said. 'Everything quieted down considerably after that.'

Jesse noticed the holes in the wall, one on either side of the fireplace.

'Am I allowed to speak?' Billy Singer said.

Molly walked over and picked up the guns.

'Before you do,' Jesse said to Singer, 'maybe you can explain what you're doing here together. Ed and you. Since we're all under the impression that the two of you get along about as well as cats in a sack. And I've heard each of you talk endless shit about the other.'

'Why aren't you arresting him?' Barrone said, pointing at Crow. 'He's the one who walked in and started waving a gun around.'

'Due time,' Jesse said. 'And for the time *being*, I'm talking to our host.'

'Host this,' Billy Singer said.

Jesse sighed.

'Did you invite Ed here?' Jesse said.

'As a matter-of-fact I did,' Singer said.

'And why is that?' Jesse said.

'None of your business,' Barrone said.

'I could shoot him, you want,' Crow said.

Jesse turned back to Singer. 'You were saying?'

'I just decided,' Singer said, 'that with everything going on in this town all of a sudden, maybe the best thing was for us to stop talking at each other in the media and just go to neutral corners before somehow this whole thing becomes even more of a shitshow than it already is and we lose the people on the Board who want the thing to go through.'

'A reasonable enough sentiment,' Molly said.

Barrone looked at her as if he'd forgotten she was still in the room.

'I was talking to your boss,' he said to Molly. Dismissively. At least she didn't shoot him.

'Same as talking to me,' Jesse said.

Crow had his own gun at his side, pointing at the floor. Jesse could have asked for it, but he knew it would only be for show, and to make Singer and Barrone and the two mutts feel better about things.

'Anyway, it's what we were talking about when Cochise burst through the door,' Barrone said.

Singer said to Crow, 'What the hell were you even doing here in the first place?'

'I was following Big Ed here for the fun of it,' Crow said.

'Because you're such a fun guy,' Singer said.

Crow ignored him. 'Then Mister Ed shows up, after I've listened to him talk the same shit you have. So I got the idea that somehow you've been playing me, Billy. And then, as an added bonus, I found out that two guys who might be the two guys shot at the chief and me the other night might very well be working for you.'

'I got no idea what you're talking about, but if I did, I'd tell you that I hit what I aim at, asshole,' one of the guys on the floor said.

'Shut up,' the other one said.

'You send these two geniuses to search Neil O'Hara's house tonight?' Jesse said.

'I've got no idea what you're talking about, or why I'd even want to know that,' Singer said. 'This thing has gotten too hot and I finally decided to bring in Sammy and Roy here as bodyguards.'

'Or really shitty home invaders,' Crow said.

'Blow me,' one of the guys on the floor said.

'You believe what you want to, Stone,' Singer said. 'But this *was* a business meeting. All this has ever been from the start is a business trip for me. I don't know anything about houses getting broken into, or Neil O'Hara, or the dead tree hugger or anything else. And if you don't have any other questions, I'd appreciate you getting the hell out of my house.'

He started to say something else, but stopped himself.

'A big Vegas hotshot like you, Billy,' Crow said. 'Now I'm wondering if you're looking for a way to run some kind of side game.'

'And just how do I plan to do that?' Singer said.

'Don't know yet,' Crow said, 'but if you are, one of us will figure it out.'

'*Us?*' Molly said.

Jesse turned to her and said, 'Relieve Mr Cromartie of his weapon, and then cuff him.'

'Finally,' Ed Barrone said.

Crow handed Molly his gun, and turned his back to her.

'You have the right to remain silent,' Molly said.

'I think of it more as a privilege,' Crow said.

34

'You buying that kumbaya shit with Billy and Barrone?' Crow said.

Jesse snorted.

'Oh, wait,' he said. 'You're being serious.'

Well past three in the morning now. They were in Jesse's office. Molly had gone home a few minutes ago, saying she'd had as much fun hanging around with the boys tonight as a girl could stand.

'Thanks for having my back,' Crow said to her as she was leaving.

'I had *his* back,' she said, jutting her chin at Jesse.

Crow shrugged. "Night, Molly,' he said.

"Night, Wilson,' she said.

'You two seem to have a nice healthy dialogue going there,' Jesse said when she was gone.

'She acts like I did something to her she didn't want done,' Crow said.

'Too much information,' Jesse said.

'Just telling you how I see it,' Crow said. 'It was something *we* did, not just something one of us did to the other.'

'Son of a bitch,' Jesse said. 'I think you done cracked the case.'

'Women,' Crow said.

'Not all,' Jesse said. 'Just this one.'

They sat in silence then. By now Jesse knew that Crow was

even more comfortable with silence than he was. No small thing.

'I still don't trust you,' Jesse said to him.

'And proud of it, I'll bet,' Crow said.

'And you no longer trust Billy Singer.'

'I never trusted him,' Crow said. 'I just had my own deal with him, if he got the land. He promised me a small piece.'

'Generous,' Jesse said. 'You believed him?'

He told Jesse what Singer had told him about how he was smart enough not to screw Crow over and think he could get away with it.

'But now he fires you,' Jesse said.

Crow grinned. 'When trust is gone in a relationship,' he said.

'So what do you think Barrone was really doing there tonight?' Jesse said.

'Beats me,' Crow said. 'What I don't get is why they'd join forces.'

'And develop the land together?' Jesse said. 'These are not guys who are good at sharing.'

'I've known Billy a long time,' Crow said. 'He hates Ed Barrone as much as he hates people skimming on him.'

Jesse said, 'Maybe they only joined forces to see if they could find whatever it is those two morons were looking for at Neil's house.'

'If it was them,' Crow said. 'Or even knew that Neil *might* have something.'

'You think Singer might have been telling the truth?'

'He does that sometimes,' Crow said, 'but only as a last resort.'

Jesse put his old New Balance grays up on his desk. They looked older than he was.

'Can't have you running around town like some kind of vigilante,' Jesse said to Crow now. 'Whether you've now done me a couple solids or not.'

'"Vigilante" may be a little strong,' Crow said.

'I thought it would be insulting for me to call you a mall cop,' Jesse said.

'How about thinking of me as an unlicensed private detective?' Crow said. 'Like Sunny Randall, just without papers?'

'You know about Sunny,' Jesse said. Then added, "Course you do.'

Jesse looked at his watch. Nearly four now.

'What I don't get,' Jesse said, 'is what's in this for you?'

Crow grinned again. 'You want me to be honest with you even though you just told me you don't trust me.'

'Pretty much.'

'The girl, Blair, I met her,' he said. 'She's a sweet kid. And she loved the guy whose body just got found. And from everything I know, being around here again, is that your friend O'Hara was on the right side of this.'

'He was on the right side of most things,' Jesse said.

'But now it's like with the Francisco kid,' Crow said. 'It's not the way I came in on this thing.'

'So who's side are you on?'

Crow stood now, arching his back like he was trying to crack it, then stretching his neck one way and then the other.

Then he reached across the desk.

They shook hands.

'Your side,' Crow said, before telling Jesse that he was going to need his gun back.

35

Molly refused to accept that Blair Richmond might be dead. She was like a dog with a bone, not that Jesse would ever put it that way. So she kept looking, like she was lifting up rocks all over social media, hoping that if Blair was out there somewhere, even having gone to ground, she might have made a mistake and left a trail.

From the start she'd said she was the obvious choice for this particular detail.

'I've practically got a doctorate in social media,' she said.

'I don't remember you taking some kind of class,' Jesse said.

'I did,' she said. 'It's called daughters.'

Suit was still being stonewalled on Neil O'Hara's cell phone records, and on the landline in his office. And could find no record of Ben Gage ever having a cell phone account. What they did know, from the SOB Twitter account, taken down a few weeks ago, is that he had been receiving death threats from people who'd seen him as the biggest obstructionist on the land deal. Gabe was now tracking the ones dumb enough to leave the tweet version of breadcrumbs about their real identities. Peter Perkins, in his last few months before retirement, was helping out with that.

It was always the same, Jesse knew. Pulling on strings. Somehow he wanted to roll this all up before the vote. But they were going to need some luck. Or some breaks. Or both. Maybe he could stop the thing somehow, even though Neil couldn't.

Billy Singer's two body men waited until the afternoon to show up at the station wanting their guns back, bringing their licenses and carry permits with them. Sammy Baldelli and Roy Santo. Not from Vegas, as it turned out. Both from Rhode Island. Both with priors. Jesse couldn't prove that either one of them had been at Neil's house. But Jesse was as sure as Crow was that it had been them at the house, and then on the beach, because if it wasn't them, then who?

Jesse came out into the squad room and handed them the Berettas back himself.

He got very close to them.

'You take both the shots, Sammy?' he said. 'Or did you leave it to this genius?'

'I'm telling you, Stone,' Baldelli said, 'you've got this wrong. Somebody might have done this shit, but it wasn't us.'

'You got *us* all wrong, dumbass,' Santo said.

'Do I?' Jesse said.

He turned and grabbed the front of Santo's nylon jacket with both hands and lifted him off the ground as if he were lifting a child.

He could hear the room go silent.

'Let go of me,' Santo said.

But it wasn't easy acting tough when your feet were off the ground.

'Not just yet,' Jesse said, trying to keep any strain out of his voice.

Then he said, 'What were the two of you looking for the other night at the house?'

'I'm telling you,' Santo said, 'it wasn't us.'

'No wonder people hate cops,' Baldelli said.

Jesse put Santo down. The two of them walked out of the station. Jesse went back to his office and shut the door and sat down behind his desk and began to get his breathing under control. Only he knew how close he'd come to smacking them both. That feeling, the rising high heat that all cops knew and all had to keep under control and only some did, could come on him as powerfully as the urge to take a drink.

He took his mitt and his ball out of the bottom drawer and began fiercely throwing the ball into the pocket. He knew that Suit and Molly and Gabe and Peter could hear the sound of it outside. And he knew that *they* knew enough not to interrupt him when the sound of the ball in the glove was as loud as it was right now, like firecrackers going off. When he needed to blow off steam this way. Maybe Molly, across the room, had seen it in his eyes when he'd grabbed Roy Santo.

The ball had actually put a familiar sting in the palm of his left hand, just because the pocket of the old glove was so threadbare by now. But there was still such a loud, singing sound in his ears that he almost didn't hear his phone.

No caller ID.

Jesse knew surprisingly few people who had that on their phones.

When he answered he heard, 'Yeah.'

Vinnie. His usual greeting.

Jesse waited.

'I got something maybe on your boy Singer,' Vinnie Morris said.

36

Jesse asked where he was. Vinnie said, 'Vegas still.' Jesse asked where in Vegas and Vinnie said his suite at The Mirage. Jesse asked if he was paying. Vinnie snorted and said that was a good one, no shit.

Then he suggested that they have their conversation on what he called 'The Zoom.'

Jesse laughed.

'*Zoom?*' he said. 'Is this really you?'

'I tried The Zoom out the other day,' he said. 'Got a kick out of it, not gonna lie. More like real talking.'

'And you such a talker,' Jesse said.

'Stop talking and gimme your email address and I'll send you the link,' Vinnie said.

A few minutes later there they were on each other's screens. It looked like some suite behind Vinnie. Jesse pointed that out.

'Prepaid,' Vinnie said.

Jesse said he was happy for him, but what did he have on Singer?

'Yeah,' Vinnie said. 'So the guy I'm here for, he knows the

guy. Singer, I mean. And my guy says that Singer has some major problems, all about to collide.'

Jesse said, 'Not to get you off point. But does that drink next to you have an umbrella in it?'

'Maybe I shoulda done this on the phone,' Vinnie said, 'upon further review.'

'You've come a long way from Joe Broz and Gino Fish,' Jesse said.

'You wanna hear me out or not?'

It came out 'he-ah.'

Vinnie took him through it then, in his spare, linear way. Like a lot of guys in Vegas, Billy Singer had gotten crushed by COVID-19, and still wasn't close to coming all the way back at The House, not with gambling, not with occupancy at the hotel, or his restaurants, or retail.

'Basically revenue's still down half, maybe a little more, maybe a little less, depending on the month,' Vinnie said.

'But like you said,' Jesse said, 'isn't he in the same boat as everybody else out there?'

He heard a doorbell in the background then, saw Vinnie's head jerk to the side before he yelled, 'You think that *Do Not Disturb* sign is some kind of poker bluff?'

Turned back to the screen. 'Where were we?'

'I just asked you why Billy's troubles are worse than everybody else's.'

'Because everybody else don't have Billy's loans, which need to be paid off, like yesterday,' Vinnie said.

Vinnie told Jesse the name of Billy's bank, and asked if he'd heard of it. Jesse said that even people in outer space knew the name of that particular bank by now. Vinnie stopped and asked Jesse how much he understood about high finance. Jesse said the reason his son was doing his taxes now was because he didn't even have a good handle on low finance.

He saw Vinnie sip his drink, which looked to be the color of his shirt. At least he didn't use the straw.

'So,' he said. 'Over the past few years, Singer has turned into a juggler. He refinances like it's going out of style every time a big principal payment is due. And he managed to stay ahead of shit until a few years ago, when he stepped in it big-time and personally guaranteed the loans with the bank whose name everybody knows by now.'

'And now that bank finally wants its money,' Jesse said.

'But he don't have it,' Vinnie said. 'He's got enough to cover him on this deal back there, if he gets the land. He's got enough for that, but not the loans. He's held them off so far, but can't for much longer, and when they come after him, they're not just gonna take the hotel and the casino. They will cut his nuts off with personal bankruptcy. And from everything I know, Singer would cut his own nuts off before he'd go down for that in front of the whole freaking world.'

'So he needs the land, and all the side deals he'll be able to make with construction and developers that'll come with it,' Jesse said.

'Needs it like this town needs suckers,' Vinnie said.

'This helps a lot,' Jesse said.

'I ain't done,' Vinnie said. 'On account of it gets better, just not better for this schmuck. Turns out, according to my guy, that our Billy is also a tax cheat, with all the usual high-roller dodges that go with that. Deductions for consulting charges.' He put air quotes around *consulting*. 'Because of course he's got his deadbeat kids on the payroll, too.'

'Don't they all,' Jesse said.

'My guy says that cheating the government is all tied up with dirty money overseas,' Vinnie said. 'So the poor bastard doesn't just have the bank on his ass, he's got the IRS.'

Vinnie sipped the pink drink. On their Zoom call.

'He'd be better off with me on his ass,' Vinnie said. 'Bottom line? This guy's needing this deal this much makes him dangerous as hell.'

'When we last spoke,' Jesse said, 'you told me Barrone was the guy I needed to watch.'

'It's a fluid situation,' Vinnie said.

Jesse saw him check his phone. Put it down. 'We done?' Vinnie said.

'One more,' Jesse said. 'Ask your guy the next time you talk to him if he thinks Singer would be desperate enough to cut some kind of side deal with Barrone.'

'I can answer that one after listening to all this shit on Singer out here,' Vinnie said. 'He'd get into bed with an iguana to save his ass.'

'One more.'

Vinnie said, 'You already did one more.'

'You ever hear of a couple of hitters from Rhode Island named Sammy Baldelli and Roy Santo?'

Vinnie had been reaching for his screen. He stopped.

'Them two are in this?'

'With Singer,' Jesse said. 'I assumed he imported them.'

Vinnie said, 'They're from Albert Antonioni's old crew. You know him?'

'Sunny did.'

'Them two were the worst,' Vinnie said.

'Killers?' Jesse said.

'Only for the sheer enjoyment of it,' Vinnie said.

It came out 'she-ah.'

'Forewarned is forearmed,' Jesse said.

'Make sure it's a lot of arms,' Vinnie said.

Then he said 'Later' and was gone.

37

At eight the next morning, Jesse sat in Neil O'Hara's old office, across Neil's antique desk, the one he used to joke to Jesse was old enough to be indigenous. He'd been ordered here by Gary

Armistead, who'd informed Jesse when he'd awakened him that he was pulling rank, and Jesse just had to deal with that.

Armistead had been so loud and so angry since Jesse had sat down that Jesse had begun to worry about the possibility of spontaneous combustion.

The source of the combustion being Jesse himself.

'You thought it was a good idea to get up in Singer's ass,' he said, 'and Ed Barrone's? On the same night? Well, guess what? Now I'm up in yours.'

'And, boy, if I find out about it,' Jesse said.

'Is that supposed to be funny?' Armistead said.

'Guess not,' Jesse said.

Armistead would occasionally get up and pace behind the oversized desk, but staying at the top of his voice. For now he was back in his chair. It was the one piece of furniture in Neil's old office he'd changed. The chair looked to Jesse like one of those fancy ergonomic deals Molly was always on him to try.

'Are you trying to get me to fire you?' Armistead said.

'For doing my job?' Jesse said. 'Deputy Chief Crane and I were investigating an active-shooter incident.'

'You were there to bust balls and you know it,' Armistead said.

'It *is* one of Deputy Chief Crane's specialties,' Jesse said. 'Just not in this case. We were responding to a call from a neighbor about shots having been fired at Singer's house.'

'*Shots fired by your Indian friend!*'

'Not very politically correct for a politician,' Jesse said.

'And when you do show up, you talk to Singer and Barrone like they're the criminals,' Armistead said. 'And then, the frosting on the cake, you let your friend, this Crow guy, walk.'

'We didn't have enough to hold him.'

'Don't give me that shit,' Armistead said. 'You know what I ought to do? I ought to suspend you until the Board votes so you don't find a way to jack the whole thing up.'

'I thought the whole thing was a foregone conclusion,' he said.

'It will be if you don't get in the way,' Armistead said. He shook his head. 'I really should just fire you and come up with a reason later.'

Jesse smiled.

'Do it,' he said.

'Don't tempt me.'

'Sounds like I already tempted you,' Jesse said. 'So do what you have to do, Gary. Set me down and then explain to your brand-new constituents *why* you set me down in the middle of an investigation about the death of your predecessor.'

Armistead started to say something. Jesse held up a hand.

'You know who maybe turned out to be a big winner with Neil O'Hara dead?' Jesse continued. 'The guy with great big ambition who replaced him.'

'You said you were just doing your job last night? I'm doing mine, and looking out for what's best for the town,' Armistead said. 'Now get the hell out of my office.'

'Funny,' Jesse said. 'I can't stop thinking of it as Neil's office.'

'You have to know this isn't over,' Gary Armistead said.

'Finally we agree on something,' Jesse said.

When he was walking back to the station, he thought that the new mayor had talked about getting up in Jesse's ass, but that any fair-minded person would have had to conclude that it had been the other way around.

38

Jesse and Molly were finishing dinner in his office, wood-fired pizza from the Gull now that Spike had installed his new oven in the extension to the kitchen he'd had built.

Molly said that pizza was pizza. Jesse told her that even cops could get arrested for throwing around irresponsible language like that.

She had spent most of her time over the green pepper and mushroom pie telling him that he was making a mistake trusting Crow. He told her what he'd told Crow. That he didn't trust him.

'You practically *have* deputized him,' Molly said. 'Do you honestly believe he's in this because he wants to help you? There's always an angle.'

'When you say "angle,"' he said, 'I assume you don't mean horizontal.'

She gave him a look that had never meant anything good for him, but held her fire.

'Bottom line is that I think he can help,' Jesse said. 'He already *has* helped, and you know it.'

'You'll be sorry,' she said, and then added, 'Like I am.'

'You need to let things go,' he said.

'Look who's talking,' she said.

He changed the subject, asking when Michael would be back. She said in a week or so, that the boss, Teddy Altman, wanted to make a quick side trip to Paris to visit a boat-building company there that was supposed to be one of the best in the world. Jesse said Molly would be less cranky when Michael was back. She accused him of being a sexist pig and snapped that she wasn't cranky. Jesse said she sure sounded cranky.

It went like that for a few minutes, the two of them once again sounding like an old bickering married couple, before they cleaned up and walked outside to the back lot and got into their cars.

Jesse drove to The Throw, where everything had started. Where he'd found the mayor of Paradise, his friend and left-handed first baseman, dead because of a single shot fired into his right temple.

He didn't know whether Neil had died here or had been moved here, and might never know.

What had Neil died knowing?

He kept coming back to that. Where else? Did he know what Ben Gage knew? Something else Jesse might never know.

Jesse walked back to the grave where he'd found Neil, the sound of the ocean behind him and the sound of night birds all around him.

He was finally walking back to the Explorer when his phone rang.

He took it out of the side pocket of his jacket.

Unknown Caller

He wondered if Vinnie Morris might have turned up something new on Billy Singer when he heard the scared, weak voice of Kate O'Hara, sounding as if it were about to shatter.

'Jesse… please help me.'

39

He kept her on the phone as he headed for the bridge to Stiles Island, after asking her if she needed him to call for an ambulance. She said she did not. He asked if she was sure. Kate said she was.

'Just hurry,' she said.

'What happened?' Jesse said.

'I walked in on them…' she said. Her voice trailed off for a moment. 'They must have been looking for… something… One of them hit me.'

She was waiting for him on the porch when he came around the corner. She was holding something to the side of her face, probably ice. As Jesse ran up the walk he saw her start to slide down the doorframe before he got to her in time.

He started to walk her into the house when she dropped the icepack suddenly and turned and put her arms around him.

'I'm so sorry,' Kate said.

'Don't be,' he said.

Then he pulled back and got an arm around her shoulder and got her into the living room and sat her down on the sofa. There were books from the built-in case scattered all over the floor and cushions and a lamp turned over, and one of the end tables near the sofa. The room had been tossed.

'Is the whole house like this?' Jesse said.

'The downstairs,' she said. 'I haven't been upstairs.'

'Doorbell cam didn't help?' he said.

'They must have come through the kitchen door,' she said.

Jesse walked back there. He could see where somebody had broken one of the windows, probably unlocked the door that way. There was glass all over the floor.

He went back to the front door now, picked up the icepack where she'd dropped it, came back and handed it to her. He could see the bruising starting to show from her right cheekbone all the way down her jawline.

'Not sure ice is going to help at this point,' she said.

'As an old ballplayer,' Jesse said, 'let me tell you that it never hurts.'

'Not much of a face right now,' she said.

'Still a nice one,' he said.

He asked her if she wanted a drink. She said not right now. He asked if they'd hit her more than once and she said no, she'd just hit her head again on the floor when she went down.

'You should be seen by a doctor,' Jesse said. 'That new Urgent Care over here is just a few blocks away.'

'I'm fine,' she said, then added, 'At least now I am.'

'Not much evidence of that,' he said.

'If my head still hurts in the morning, I'll go see somebody,' she said. 'For now, as they say, it only hurts when I laugh, so I feel as if I'm in no immediate danger.'

She took him through it. She'd felt a need for the ribs at the Gull, so she'd decided to do takeout, because she didn't want to go over there and sit alone. Too much alone time these days, she said. Then she managed to build a small smile and said, 'But who knows more about alone time than you, Jesse.'

She had locked the house before she left, she was sure of that. The front door was still locked when she got back from the Gull. She heard a noise upstairs as soon as she walked in.

'They must have seen you leave,' Jesse said.

'Then I was like one of those silly girls in the horror movies, actually asking if someone was here,' she said. 'The next thing I remember is someone coming from my right, out of the den, and punching me in the face.'

He thought she might cry, but she didn't.

'No one has punched me in my face my whole life,' she said.

'So there was more than one of them.'

'I'm sure I heard somebody upstairs,' she said. 'But if there was somebody up there, I didn't see him. I wish I could tell you more, I'm sorry.'

'Stop apologizing, Kate,' Jesse said. 'Do you feel as if you lost consciousness?'

'I don't think so,' she said. 'The next thing I remember is one of them pressing my face to the floor and asking me if he'd left it with me.' She ran a hand through her hair. 'Left *what*, Jesse?'

'Somebody is looking for something that might interfere with the sale of the land,' Jesse said. 'They've searched the house of Ben Gage from Save Our Beach, the kid that just got shot over in Marshport. Somebody searched Neil's house the other night. Couple guys. I knew someone was in there because I'd left a sensor the last time I'd been there. They ended up shooting at me before I lost them on the beach.'

'Why would they think Neil would tell me?' she said. 'Or leave something that important with me? Do you even know exactly what it is?'

'Just something of value to one of the people involved in this deal,' Jesse said. 'Or maybe all of them.'

'But what?'

'Working on it,' he said.

'On a mission, you mean.'

'Idle hands,' Jesse said.

He asked again if he could drive her to Urgent Care. She told him no again. Jesse said that she was as stubborn as Molly Crane, likely slugged by the same guys. Kate said she'd take that as a compliment. She said she'd take that drink now. Scotch. Jesse asked where she kept it. She said on the kitchen counter, in a corner underneath the cupboards. Jesse went into the kitchen and saw it was as much of a mess as the living room. There were two bottles. One was red wine.

The other was Chivas Regal.

He picked it up and saw that it was mostly full. Always a happy moment for him in his drinking days. Seeing the amber liquid nearly all the way to the top. Feeling the weight of the bottle. He stared at it a moment longer, then found a glass and uncapped the bottle and poured scotch into it.

He couldn't remember the last time he'd had his hand around a bottle of scotch. He screwed the cap back on and made sure not to smell it. He already knew what it smelled like. He could teach a master class in what it smelled like and what it tasted like. And felt like.

'Jesse?' Kate called from the living room. 'You find it okay?'

Her voice snapped him out of it. He slid the bottle back into the corner, thinking that no bad guy he had ever encountered had ever been more dangerous to him than the glass in his hand. It had nearly cost him everything, including Kate once.

But he'd made it through another day without pouring himself a drink.

Or had almost made it.

Day wasn't quite over.

He went back to the living room and handed her the glass

and she drank some. The bruise on her face was darkening. He told her to stay where she was. She said she wasn't going anywhere. He went through the house then, room by room, downstairs and upstairs. When she walked in on them, they must just have been going through the upstairs rooms, because there were just a few drawers pulled out of her dresser, and they seemed to not have made it to her clothes closet. Jesse was sure they'd left no prints behind. If it was the same two guys, they hadn't left prints at either Ben Gage's house or Neil's, either.

But was it the same two guys? Or were there roving teams of idiots involved in this thing? Maybe Ed Barrone had one of his own. And Lawton's goon had chased Ben Gage and Blair Richmond that time.

When he came back downstairs Kate had curled herself into a corner of the couch, feet underneath her. Most of the scotch was gone.

'You're sure you didn't get any kind of look at them?' Jesse said.

She shook her head.

'If they're who I think they are,' he said, 'they work for Billy Singer.'

He was sitting next to her on the couch. He was sure he was imagining that he could smell the scotch. He grinned at her.

'What I don't know right now,' he said, 'could fill up Fenway Park.'

He took out his phone.

'Who are you calling?' she said.

'The station,' he said. 'I want them to send a car over here and have it stay until morning. Do you want me to file a report?'

'I don't have what they wanted,' she said. 'What would be the point?'

She stared at Jesse now with what he thought had always been truly amazing eyes. Beautiful eyes. Beautiful woman. They suddenly seemed closer to each other than they actually were.

'Why can't you stay?' she said finally.

His throat felt thick suddenly.

'Because I can't,' he said.

'Just as a friend,' she said.

'Neil was my friend,' he said.

'Mine, too,' she said.

'He was mine longer,' Jesse said.

She was right there. Her and the scotch. Like old times.

He held her eyes for a long time.

Then he said, 'You want me to help you clean up?'

'I'll do it in the morning,' she said.

'You're sure you'll be all right?' he said.

'Under the watchful eyes of the Paradise Police Department,' Kate said, 'who wouldn't be?'

'I meant being alone,' he said.

She smiled with her eyes one last time and said, 'One of these days I really *might* be as good at it as you are.'

When he got to the Explorer, the squad car with Peter Perkins in it having just arrived, he took big, deep breaths of the night ocean air. Then he got inside, started up the engine, and called Crow.

40

They were on Jesse's terrace. Crow was sipping whiskey out of a flask he carried with him sometimes. Jesse drank decaf coffee. He planned to get some sleep tonight. Just not quite yet.

'Tell me again what time she called you,' Crow said.

Jesse did.

'Then I don't see how it could have been them,' Crow said. 'They were getting a load on at the Scupper then. You want to lock them up? Send somebody over there and have them wait outside, and get 'em on a DUI. They're probably still there, getting dumber by the minute.'

'Be a challenge,' Jesse said.

'You ever think about how much of your life you've spent banging up against guys like them?' Crow said.

'You were a guy like them,' Jesse said.

Crow capped the flask and stuck it in his back pocket.

'For all you know,' Crow said, 'I still might be.'

'There's that,' Jesse said.

'One of the things that keeps our relationship fresh,' Crow said.

'How'd you know they were at the Scupper?' Jesse said. 'You follow them tonight?'

'Got some money out,' Crow said. 'Here and Marshport. With bartenders mostly. The two morons show up someplace, I get a call.'

'Saves money on gas,' Jesse said.

They could hear the ocean from here, but not see it.

'If it's not them,' Crow said, 'that means we've got two more headbangers to worry about.'

Jesse told him he'd taken the words right out of his mouth.

Crow had his boots up on the railing. Jesse said, 'What kind of boots are those? I used to wear boots back in L.A., thought it made me look like more of a hard case.'

'Lucchese,' Crow said. 'Not cheap, but I've had them awhile. You get them broken in right, you stay with them.'

'Like a baseball glove,' Jesse said. 'I still have the last one I used as a player.'

'It still bother you, the way it ended?' Crow said. 'Baseball, I mean.'

Jesse was about to ask him how he knew how baseball had ended for him, but it was as if he were reading his mind because he said, 'Molly told me.'

'It only bothers me most days,' Jesse said. 'And every night.'

'I never had anything that mattered to me like that,' Crow said.

'You act like you do now.'

'Doesn't take much pretending when I think about that girl.'

'Why'd she get to you this way?'

''Cause that shit with the land mattered to her the way playing ball mattered to you,' Crow said.

They sat in silence, staring into the night.

'I'm still stuck on the same things,' Jesse said. 'Who needs the deal the most. And what the hell they're looking for.'

Then he told Crow about the extent of Billy Singer's money problems. Crow said he had no idea, when he'd signed on he just looked at Singer and saw every other high-roller asshole in Vegas.

'He's no better or different than Barrone,' Crow said. 'Barrone's just the stiff who's local.'

'Maybe we need to know just how hard Barrone got hit by the virus,' Jesse said. 'Guys like them, there's no vaccine gets them back all the money they lost.'

'You or me?' Crow said.

'There's somebody I want to talk to, might know.'

'What about Lawton?' Crow said. 'You add it all up, he might need it more than either Billy or Barrone. He only gets to be a higher roller than he is already if he gets his money.'

'If it's not Baldelli and Santo,' Jesse said, 'be nice to know who sent somebody to Kate O'Hara's house.'

'You want it to be Baldelli and Santo.'

'Something else we need to consider?' Jesse said. 'That maybe they're not the only two morons Billy's got on the payroll.'

He saw Crow grin. '"We,"' he said.

Crow stood. He said he could call the Scupper and see if Baldelli and Santo were still there, and rout them just for sport. Jesse said to leave them be for now, and hope that they drank themselves into comas.

Jesse stood. They both hung over the railing.

'You seem to trust me pretty good for a guy you say you don't trust,' Crow said.

'Funny world,' Jesse said.

'Can't have guys running around town beating up women,' Crow said.

'Place is going to hell,' Jesse said.

He turned to look at Crow, silhouetted against the night sky, like he was a part of it.

'One of these days they might come after us,' Crow said. 'You know that, right?'

'I kind of look forward to it,' he said.

Crow grinned.

'Same,' he said.

41

The next afternoon Jesse was in Dorchester, sitting in the office of a man named Mike Altamero.

The office was off Morrissey Boulevard, past the old *Boston Globe* building that Sunny had pointed out to Jesse one time when they were driving to the Cape for a romantic weekend, when they were still having those.

This was the modest home of Altamero Construction. Jesse had been reading back on Ed Barrone in his spare time, trying to find something in his past that might make him as desperate as the money-strapped Billy Singer to close the deal on The Throw.

Altamero, fittingly enough, was built like a block of concrete. Dark complexion, short hair a mixture of gray and white, big hands he'd probably used to build his business.

Mike Altamero had been in serious competition with Ed

Barrone for the casino that eventually got built in Taunton, until Altamero suddenly withdrew his bid at the last moment. When he'd been asked why by a reporter from the *Globe*, Altamero had said, 'You gotta know when to fold 'em.' Other than that, he had never said another public word about it.

Now Jesse said to him, 'Doesn't look as if Barrone's going to be as lucky with Billy Singer.'

'Luck ain't got anything to do with it,' Altamero said.

'What does that mean?'

'It means that Barrone ain't going to be able to put the muscle on Singer the way he did me,' Altamero said. 'Just following the thing, it looks like more of a fair fight between them two.'

'Put the muscle on you how?' Jesse said.

'He beat up my kid, that's how, the son of a bitch,' Altamero said. 'Or had him beat up. Same difference. Coming out of Santarpio's one night. You know Santarpio's? Best pizza on the planet.'

Jesse said he had a friend who'd taken him there. She'd told him the same thing about the pizza before they went. And hadn't lied.

'They tried to make it look like a mugging,' Altamero said. 'Even went through the motions of stealing Mikey's wallet. But I knew better.'

Altamero grabbed a coffee mug that looked as small as a shot glass in his right hand.

'And Mikey, he's a tough kid, like I raised him,' Altamero said. 'Played linebacker at Northeastern. One of the guys holding him while the other one smacked him around said, "You know what this is about."'

'What did you do?'

'Went looking for him, is what I did. I mean, fuck that shit. Barrone denied it, of course. Said he didn't do business that way, even though we both knew that's *exactly* how he does business. But before I left his office, he told me that every deal requires risk assessment, on both sides, and he wondered if I'd properly assessed my risk. That was before he had a couple of his body men show me out.'

'Why does he want the land in my town so badly?' Jesse said.

'Because the word on the street is that the guy is underwater, on account of what he's lost the last couple years,' Altamero said. 'And all's I can say is that it couldn't happen to a nicer guy. I hope he chokes on his own debt.'

'The word on the street,' Jesse said.

He always wanted to ask, *which* street?

'I hear that he was looking for loans at a couple of the banks that have been kissing his fat ass for years,' Altamero said. 'But he got turned down flat when he went to them a few months ago, around that time that land got put up for sale.'

'Can he get the land in our town without a loan?' Jesse said.

'There's always other ways.'

Jesse told him then about Billy Singer's current circumstances, electing to leave out the part about the Feds.

'Two losers in the same boat,' Altamero said. 'A boat that sounds like it's taking on water.'

'But they've both got enough money to buy the land,' Jesse said.

'Barely, I'm guessing,' Altamero said. 'But once they're across the goal line, then the money starts coming in from all the contractors and golf course builders and retailers want to be in business with them. At which, if it's Barrone, he stops being sideways with the banks, and everybody lives happily ever after.'

'What happens if the whole deal goes sideways?' Jesse said to Altamero.

'What I hear, that ain't possible, the train's too far down the track.'

'But say that it does,' Jesse said. 'From what I hear, Singer might not get whole even if he wins the bid.'

'Why's that?'

'Not at liberty.'

'I don't talk,' Altamero said, 'even after Barrone done what he done to my kid.'

Jesse said, 'Take Singer out of it. What would happen to Barrone if he loses, or if this thing falls apart?'

'Again, I'm just going on what I hear, but the bank takes the casino in Taunton, at the very least,' Altamero said. 'Or he scrambles by rolling an eleven. Like in Chapter Eleven.'

Altamero leaned forward across his desk, his thick fingers interlocked.

'You're the chief up there,' he said. 'This ain't just about the land, is it?'

'It is not,' Jesse said. 'A couple people are dead because of this.'

'One of them the mayor,' Altamero said.

'He was a friend of mine,' Jesse said.

Almatero gave him a long look. 'You don't let shit go, do you?'

'Hardly ever,' Jesse said.

'Well, all's I can tell you is that I hope Barrone goes down for whatever he can go down on,' Altamero said.

Jesse nodded.

'Karma's a bitch, ain't it?' Mike Altamero said.

'So I've heard,' Jesse said.

42

Jesse had no interest in fighting the rush-hour traffic heading north at this time of day. He'd called Kate O'Hara again to ask how she was feeling. She said she was feeling the same as she had when he'd called her in the morning.

He thought about asking her to meet him for dinner at the Gull if she was feeling up to it. The words were nearly out of his mouth before he swallowed them. He had been too close to something happening between them last night before an inner alarm sounded. What Dix called his moral alarm, one that Dix had suggested could survive a nuclear attack. So he had left. Even now it amused the hell out of Jesse that he'd chosen the company, and companionship, of Crow over a woman with whom he once might have been about half in love.

He got off the expressway in Chinatown, and eventually made his way to Charles Street, which ran between the Public Garden and the Boston Common, finally making a left at the Charles Street Meeting House and a right on River Street Place until he parked the Explorer in front of Sunny Randall's house.

A famous writer had basically given it to her, not rent-free, but close enough, considering the neighborhood. He had walked these streets with her more times than he could recall. They had even gone across the little bridge and run together along the Charles, then come back to the house at the end of the street and made love in the big bed upstairs.

Jesse knew he'd never been in love with Kate O'Hara, not really, as many times as he'd tried to talk himself into believing that he was.

It was Sunny he'd been in love with, and still was, not that it was doing him much good lately.

Don't project. Another of the big ones from AA. So Jesse wasn't projecting that it was over between him and Sunny. It just felt that way right now. Had she said she'd call when they'd last spoken? He felt like she had. But hadn't called. No idea what was happening with her in L.A., or when she'd be back, and whether or not they'd pick up where they'd left off. He asked himself again: _What are you, in high school?_

Sitting outside your girlfriend's house, or ex-girlfriend, or whatever she currently was, even knowing she wasn't there.

He sat there for a long time, anyway, and was about to leave when Spike came out with Rosie, Sunny's dog, on a leash. He grinned when he saw Jesse step out of the Explorer.

'I can't be extradited to Paradise, right?' Spike said.

'I'll ask the questions,' Jesse said, and walked over and shook Spike's hand.

'I'm just a gay man picking up more toys for a small dog,' he said. 'Is that a crime?'

'Should be.'

'Well, that's my excuse,' Spike said. 'What's yours?'

'In the neighborhood.'

'Yeah, sure,' Spike said. 'Jesus, you look like you miss her more than the dog does.'

Spike had grown a beard since the last time Jesse had seen him at the Gull. But he looked ripped, as always, like he ought to be starring in one of those gym ads on television. Orange T-shirt, tight, sneakers to match the shirt, skinny jeans.

'You talk to her?' Jesse said.

'Not much,' Spike said. 'And when we do, it's mostly about the dog. I don't know much about this case, but it seems to be pretty intense.'

'For her, there's never any other kind.'

'Have you talked to her?' Spike said.

'Maybe a week ago, just to check in,' Jesse said. 'Not for long.'

Spike smiled. 'You want to stand here and keep talking about her without really talking about her?' he said.

'I'd rather try to zigzag my way across Storrow Drive when the rush-hour traffic picks up,' Jesse said.

They were out of things to say. They both knew it. Jesse said he'd see him in Paradise. Spike said that always sounded kind of bleak to him.

'I miss her, too,' Spike said, 'if that's any consolation to you.'

'It's not,' Jesse said.

43

Molly thought: *How had this happened?*

Jesse and Crow had practically turned into one of those movies with a couple buddy cops. The only problem, from where she sat, was that only one of them *was* a cop. The other guy, whatever Molly's history with him – *brief* history – was one the cop had tried to put away.

Am I jealous?

Of Crow hanging out with my boss?

Not just my boss, but my best friend?

Jesse was the one always telling her that the best thing was for her to stay away from Crow, like he was trying to keep her out of harm's way. And Jesse had told her that he'd made it clear to Crow that he wanted him to steer clear of Molly as much as possible.

Now Jesse had done everything except give Crow a badge. The two of them might be together right now, as far as she knew. Sitting with their feet on Jesse's desk, chopping things up.

And I wish I was with them, Molly thought. No way around that. 'What is this, high school?' Jesse would say sometimes, often when he was talking about Sunny Randall.

Now Molly felt like she was the one in high school, and hadn't been invited to a party, even if it was just a party of two. She knew she could check her phone to see where Jesse was right now. She had done it plenty of times before. But tonight it would make her feel as if she were stalking him.

Stalking *them.*

She was alone in the house. Michael had gotten a message to her, from the boat, that he expected to be back in ten days, but probably not sooner. Michael: her husband, who she loved, and who would never know that she had cheated on him with a criminal and still imagined herself doing it again, at least in her weaker moments. Ones that would often come at this time of night.

She thought about making herself a drink. That might calm her down. Only she didn't want to calm down, damn it! She wanted to be angry with them for leaving her out.

But Molly knew her anger tonight was about more than that, or about them. She had become obsessed with her inability to find Blair Richmond, or to find out what had happened to her.

Blair Richmond, who *was* somebody's daughter.

She had been working this particular missing-persons case as hard as she'd ever worked one in her life, reaching out to every agency except the Justice League of America. From the start, Molly had been working it as if the girl – she couldn't think of her in any other way – were still alive. She refused to dwell on the alternative. In her mind Blair was out there somewhere, hiding and scared and alone.

Molly had called her high school friends. And classmates from the University of Rhode Island she could track down. She had circled back to the other members of Save Our Beach, all of them scared out of their wits themselves, looking for anything they remembered that could provide a lead.

You know what a good cop you are.

Be one now.

Molly knew that she herself couldn't do anything about saving the land, or the beach, or the town, or bringing back Ben Gage or Neil O'Hara. Making everything the way it was. But she could save this girl.

Only if she could find her.

No one had heard from her. There had been no activity on her credit card or bank card. No Venmo transfers to her or from her, at least before today. By now Molly was convinced that Blair's original cell phone was long gone, discarded or destroyed, by her or somebody else.

Molly knew how hard it was to go completely off the grid in the modern world. Blair Richmond, if she *were* still alive, had managed to do just that. It was easy enough for Molly to know why, realize what she was thinking:

They killed my boyfriend and now they're coming for me.

They. Whoever they were. Blair could only think that she had to know whatever it was that had gotten Ben Gage killed. And Mayor Neil O'Hara before that. But especially Ben. They had worked together. They had lived together and been lovers. They had to assume that whatever he knew, she knew.

Whoever the fuck they were.

She was in the kitchen about an hour later, making herself a strong cup of Irish tea, when she heard her phone making its marimba noise from where she'd left it in the living room.

She picked it up and looked at the screen.

Unknown Caller

'This is Molly Crane,' she said.

Nothing.

'Hello,' she said. 'This is Molly.'

'It's me,' she heard through a bad connection. 'Blair.'

'Please come get me,' Blair Richmond said. 'Before they do.'

44

'Before who comes to get you?'

'... who killed Ben.'

It was a terrible connection.

Molly said, 'Where are you?'

For a moment Molly felt the air come out of her because she was afraid she had lost her again.

And maybe for good.

'... past Marshport,' she said. 'Almost to the state park in

Oxbow. You know where that is? Ben built us a little cabin out here.'

Molly knew where the park was. She and Michael had often taken the girls there when they were little.

'... our safe place,' Blair said. '... we know about.'

The call started to cut out.

'... never showed up...' she said.

Molly asked for the address. Blair gave it to her. Molly typed it into Waze, which told her it would take forty minutes to get there.

Blair's voice was cutting out again.

'... explain when you get here.'

'I can have the Marshport Police send a car,' Molly said.

'Just you,' Blair said.

The call broke off. Molly grabbed her Glock, knowing her Taser and flashlight and radio were in the Cherokee. As she ran to the car, she thought about calling Jesse.

But he never called her when he was going all cowboy-up, as her Red Sox used to say.

Two could play that game. Where her house was, she knew she would beat him to Oxbow even if she did call him. She would bring in Blair Richmond, somebody's daughter, herself. Bring her home. To Molly's home.

She'd tell Jesse and his new best buddy about it later.

45

It took longer than Molly thought it would. Even using Waze, she made a couple wrong turns on the narrow, two-lane roads that took you out to the state park. One time she turned too early, another time too late.

She had been trying to call Blair to give her updates on her progress, without success. Maybe the cell service out here was hit or miss, and she'd been lucky to get through to Molly in the first place. Maybe the phone had died. No point in speculating.

Just get there.

She was on Reservoir Road now, badly lit, looking for number 10. No other houses even close to the road. No house lights anywhere that Molly could see. Middle of nowhere, Molly thought. Probably the point.

She missed the small dirt road, came back. Saw the outline of a cabin maybe a hundred yards up from Reservoir Road. Molly shut off her lights, eased the Cherokee to a stop, got out of the car, quietly closed the door. The only faint light was from the moon, covered by clouds as if shades had been drawn in front of it. But no lights on, which bothered her. She was glad the Bruins hoodie she'd been wearing when Blair called was black.

Molly had the Glock in her right hand. She had shut off her phone. She stayed low to the grass, moving slowly in a crouch along the tree line. One of Jesse Stone's rules to live by: Being overly cautious had never gotten anybody killed.

Molly thought: *Maybe I should have called Jesse and Crow.*

She thought: *Why hadn't Blair been waiting out front?*

Why were *the lights off?*

Molly talked all the time about her hunches. It was a standing joke with her and Jesse and Suit. But this was more than that now. This was a deep and visceral feeling that something was very wrong here.

If you're as scared as you sounded, why are you alone at a darkened house?

There was still only the light of the moon when Molly saw the muzzle flash through the first-floor window and heard the shot.

46

Molly didn't think now, didn't fall back on procedure, just reacted, yelled 'Police!' and fired a warning shot on the run that splintered wood underneath the front-porch railing before she heard a door slam from somewhere behind the house.

She ran in that direction and saw the shape of a man running away from her, across the small backyard.

'Stop or I'll shoot!' Molly yelled.

The man turned and fired in her direction and Molly heard the bullet hit a tree behind her.

She returned fire as she came along the side of the house and thought she might have hit him. Hadn't. Then saw him dropping to the ground suddenly and rolling and coming up into a kneeling position and getting off another shot.

Molly felt the sudden, searing pain near her left shoulder then.

She had been hit, and started to go down, but didn't. Instead she stepped out from the house, two hands on the Glock, aiming low because he was still kneeling, and fired the way she had been taught at all the hours at the range, the bullet hitting him center mass.

Someday, Jesse had told her once when he went to the range with her, this shit will get real.

The shooter went down and stayed down, motionless.

Molly felt faint because of the pain in her upper arm. But she made her way with great caution across the yard. There was only the sound of night birds around her now that the shooting had stopped.

The man was on his back, the cap with a shamrock on the front turned sideways on his head, some kind of long gun on the ground next to him. Not breathing. Eyes open. Staring up at what there was of a moon.

Molly knew she might be in shock. But knew she couldn't afford that right now, that she had to power through, despite the fact that the fingers of her left hand were starting to go numb. She checked the pulse of the man in the shamrock cap to make sure. Saw the spreading wound in the middle of his chest. But no pulse. Nothing. She had shot a man dead. She didn't bother to close his eyes. She would come back for an ID later. For now she ran back around the house and through the front door, left arm flapping at her side, kept her gun in her hand as she went inside and found Blair Richmond, lying on her back, her head in its own spreading pool of blood, an exit wound over her left eye.

Molly knelt next to her, feeling as if she were kneeling in prayer, and felt her neck.

I was too late.

But somehow Blair Richmond was still alive.

She took out her phone and prayed this time to God for enough bars, saw that there were, called 911 and said this was Deputy Chief Molly Crane of the Paradise Police Department and that there were gunshot victims at 10 Reservoir Road in Oxbow, one of them still alive but needing an ambulance, and right now.

Molly didn't include herself in the number of victims. She didn't consider herself one. She sat on the floor next to Blair Richmond, afraid to move her. Afraid to look at her. Molly pulled up the sleeve of the black Bruins sweatshirt and saw that despite the fact that the blood had soaked through and made the sleeve wet and sticky, it was just a flesh wound.

Just a flesh wound.

Sure.

Like it happened to her all the time.

She went into the kitchen and finally turned on a light in the house and found a dish towel and pressed it against the wound and then went back into the living room and sat back down next to Blair and begged her not to die.

47

They were at the Emergency Room wing of Marshport General Hospital, recently renovated and expanded. Jesse. Molly. Crow.

Molly had been examined by one of the ER doctors, stitched and bandaged.

'Do you two go anywhere without each other?' Molly said now that they were in the waiting room.

'Been nice if we'd been with you earlier, all things considered,' Jesse said.

'I learned not calling for backup from the master,' Molly said.

Another ER doctor, not the one who'd treated Molly, came out now.

'How is she?' Jesse said.

'It's a miracle that she's still alive,' he said. His name-tag read R. ABRAMSON. 'Bullet went in through the left side of the back of her head, out where you saw the hole over her eye. A through-and-through. It just happens that way sometimes, for the very fortunate few, and even then maybe ten percent of people who get shot in the head like this survive. Maybe less.'

'Surgery?' Jesse said.

'Soon,' Dr Abramson said.

'Who?'

'Me,' Abramson said. He offered a small smile. 'I'm very good at this, in case you were wondering. Doing a favor for a friend tonight by filling in for her. We usually wait for an hour once we've stabilized a patient. Now we go in and see what the path was and how much damage to the brain there was. If the bullet ricochets around in there, or breaks into fragments, there's no way she survives. Truth be told, she probably would have been gone by the time she hit the floor.'

'Jesus, Mary, and Joseph,' Molly said.

Jesse said, 'Does she have a chance?'

'To live?' Abramson said. He paused. 'It might depend more on the grace of God than even the best treatment available.'

'When she does wake up,' Molly said, 'is there a chance that she can be herself?'

'You mean normal?' Dr Abramson said. He put air quotes around 'normal.'

'Yes,' Molly said. 'That's exactly what I mean.'

'We might not know for quite some time,' Abramson said. 'For now let's just be thankful that she's still with us after being shot at close range to the back of the head.'

He said it was time for him to go to work. When he was gone, Jesse's phone buzzed. Gabe Weathers calling.

'Talk to me,' Jesse said.

He listened for about a minute until Gabe Weathers ended the call. Then Jesse turned back to Molly and Crow.

'Our shooter is from Boston, an ex-cop named Richie Carr,' he said. 'Busted out finally after setting state records for excessive force. Now hiring himself out as a contract goon, one with a pretty impressive sheet in a short amount of time. Gabe talked to somebody in Boston who said that Carr, as much of a badass as he was, was a pretty good detective, especially on what Gabe called cyber-shit. Gabe found his SUV on a dirt road running parallel to Reservoir Road.'

'Somehow he found out about that cabin,' Molly said.

'Then got there first,' Jesse said.

Molly leaned her head back and closed her eyes, and suddenly looked so weak to Jesse he was surprised she didn't slide out of the chair and end up on the floor. She had shot someone dead tonight, and been shot, and found Blair Richmond after Richie Carr had shot her. For now, Blair Richmond was luckier than Neil O'Hara had been when he'd taken a bullet to the head. Maybe from the same guy, if Jesse had been right about Neil being murdered all along.

Molly opened her eyes and looked at Jesse and said, 'If I

146

had gotten there five minutes earlier I could have saved her.'

'Or could have gotten a bullet to the head yourself if you'd walked in on them,' Crow said.

'I never shot anybody before,' she said.

'I know,' Jesse said.

'He didn't give me a choice,' she said.

'They hardly ever do,' Jesse said.

'It was too late by the time I heard the shot from inside,' she said.

'She's alive, Molls,' Jesse said. 'She'd be gone if you didn't get there when you did. I've got Gabe and Suit searching the cabin as we speak.'

'Crow can drive my car back to Paradise,' Jesse said to Molly. 'I'll drive yours.'

Jesse gently helped her to her feet, knowing she had been wounded tonight in more ways than one, getting himself on her right so he could put a hand on her right shoulder and slowly lead her toward the revolving doors. There was a moment before they got there when Jesse felt her start to sag. But Molly righted herself on her own. She said they should go right to the office, there was paperwork that needed to be filed because of an officer-involved shooting. Jesse said it could wait until morning.

Crow had gotten Molly's keys out of her bag while the ER doctor was attending to her. Her Cherokee – Jesse couldn't believe they still called it that in a politically correct world – was waiting for them out front. Crow opened the door on the passenger side. Jesse eased Molly into her seat, and somehow carefully stretched the seatbelt across her and locked it in. Crow went to collect Jesse's Explorer.

After Crow brought the Explorer around, he got close to Jesse and said, 'People who haven't done it, they think they know what it's like. They don't.'

'I know,' Jesse said.

Then Jesse got behind the wheel and he and Molly began the ride back to Paradise. She was quiet for a long time.

'I never shot anybody,' she said again.

'I know,' Jesse said.

48

When Jesse got home, he called Vinnie in Vegas to tell him what had happened with Molly, wanting to know if he knew who Richie Carr was. Vinnie said he did, it was the bad cops you remembered more than the good ones.

'You got a regular *Wild Bunch* thing going in that little town a yours,' Vinnie said. 'You ever see *The Wild Bunch*? That had some serious shooting shit in it.'

Jesse told him it was a Western, which meant of course he'd seen it.

'What I'm trying to figure out is why Billy Singer, if it was him, would bring in somebody like Richie Carr if he's already got Santo and Baldelli on the ground here,' Jesse said.

'Maybe he thought that after Santo and Baldelli basically got bitch-slapped by Crow, they weren't getting it done,' Vinnie said. 'Or maybe the other guy brought in Carr.'

'Barrone,' Jesse said.

'Could be him just as easy. Or even that Lawton. I could ask around.'

'Have at it,' Jesse said.

Vinnie had suggested they use Zoom again. Jesse told him he remembered what he looked like.

'That girl gonna make it?' Vinnie said.

'Too early to tell.'

'How's Molly?'

'She's Molly,' Jesse said. 'Which means tougher than both of us.'

'Yeah.'

There was a pause at Vinnie's end and then he said, 'She put down Richie Carr. Son... of... a... bitch.'

'Not much light, she'd already been hit, she still made the shot,' Jesse said.

'I could come back, you want,' Vinnie said. 'I pretty much got this thing buttoned up.'

'Molly and Suit and I can handle this,' Jesse said. 'And my faithful companion, Crow.'

'I got no comment on that,' Vinnie said, 'on account of it ain't as if my résumé ever stopped you when you needed something.'

Jesse thanked him for the intel and told him to go get another umbrella drink.

'It was a one-off, for chrissakes,' Vinnie said.

'I thought the umbrella went nicely with your outfit,' Jesse said.

Vinnie ignored him.

'Listen, before I go, there's something else you should know about Richie Carr, if one of your cop friends from Boston didn't tell you,' he said. 'Last few years, he's been working with a partner on any sort of gun or strong-arm shit you need.'

'Got a name?'

'Sure.'

Shoo-ah.

'Darnell Woodson is the dude's name,' Vinnie said.

'Another ex-cop?'

'Ex–Tony Marcus. Except he was so much of a psycho that even Tony had to let him go before he had to have him popped.'

'You know where I might find him?' Jesse said.

'Hope that it ain't Paradise,' Vinnie said. 'But you should ask Tony. Or have Sunny ask him.'

'I'm good,' Jesse said.

'Tony's not much for cops, maybe you heard,' Vinnie said.

'I'm not like the other boys and girls,' Jesse said.

'You don't want Darnell up on you, from what I hear,' Vinnie said, 'even if you got Crow for backup.'

'Noted.'

'I got one last question 'fore I hang up,' Vinnie Morris said. 'How did one piece of land in Fancy Ass, Massachusetts, turn into this kind of goddamn gang beef?'

49

Mayor Gary Armistead and Thomas Lawton showed up in Jesse's office first thing the next morning. Armistead had the print edition of the Paradise *Town Crier* in his hand until he tossed it on Jesse's desk.

Jesse didn't even look down at it.

'Coffee?' he said.

'You don't want to get cute with me today, Stone,' Armistead said. 'I'm not in the mood.'

'Okay,' Jesse said.

'"Okay"?'

'I won't try to get cute,' Jesse said.

They took the visitor seats across from him. Jesse asked Lawton why the mayor had asked him to come along.

'As a concerned citizen,' Lawton said.

'You know why we're here,' Armistead said. 'Nellie Shofner doesn't write the story about the girl getting shot and Molly shooting that guy without you calling her.'

'It's like you wrote the story yourself,' Lawton said. 'You think we don't know who the police department source is' – he put quotes with his fingers around 'source' – 'who told her the shooting is connected to the deaths of Neil O'Hara and Ben Gage? Give me a break.'

'Seems to me that if you want to know who the source is, you should ask the reporter,' Jesse said. 'And good luck with that if you do ask, by the way.'

He sipped some of his own coffee. Third cup of the day. He was jazzed enough to picture himself walking around his desk and banging their two heads together.

He took a good, deep breath instead, holding the air in as long as he could.

'The deputy chief of this department,' he said evenly, 'was involved in a shootout last night.'

'We can read,' Lawton said.

'She took a bullet in the arm before killing her assailant,' Jesse continued. 'Then she discovered Blair Richmond inside the house, a young woman who'd just been shot in the head by this assailant. Ms. Richmond is currently hospitalized at Marshport General, and is out of what is successful brain surgery for now, but still in a coma.'

Jesse smiled now, clasped his hands together, and leaned across his desk. Amiable Chief Jesse.

'So I'd like to ask both of you gentlemen a question,' Jesse said. 'If that *isn't* front-page news, then what the *fuck* is?'

Lawton's head snapped back a little, as if Jesse had slapped him when he raised his voice. Armistead, in suit and tie, as if he thought that dressing the part was somehow a requirement of his new job, continued to glare across the desk at Jesse.

'No one is suggesting it isn't news, Stone,' he said. 'But you wanted that story out there, written the way it was written, and somehow in the paper this morning. And you know why?'

'Help me out,' Jesse said.

'Because you are going out of your way to scare the other members of the Board away from this land deal,' Armistead said, 'even at the last minute.'

'Like you're one of those tree huggers who want this *deal* to end up dead,' Lawton added.

'Not my job,' Jesse said. 'And by the way? I thought the vote was a sure thing.'

'And we aim to keep it that way,' Armistead said, 'whatever your agenda is.'

'My agenda,' Jesse said, 'involves two people dead because of this deal and a young woman about whom neither of you seem to care who might be dying.'

Jesse stood.

'Now, if you don't mind, I'd like you both to get the hell out of my office so I can get back to work,' Jesse said.

Armistead and Lawton stood.

'When this vote is over,' Armistead said to Jesse, 'and this deal *has* gone through, there is going to be a reckoning about your future.'

'Guys like you,' Lawton said, 'sometimes get the idea that they have jobs for life.'

Jesse turned and trained one last smile on him.

'Shut the fuck up, Thomas,' he said.

'You can't talk to me like that,' he said.

'Just did,' Jesse said, and walked around his desk and held the door for them until they had in fact gotten the hell out of his office.

50

Two hours later Jesse was back in Boston, in Tony Marcus's office at a bar and restaurant he owned named Buddy's Fox.

There was a decent lunch crowd in the front room. As far as Jesse could see as he walked past the bar, he was the only white person there. He was wearing a windbreaker and jeans and sneakers and his favorite old Red Sox cap. Somehow he felt as if he still could have been carrying a sign that read COP.

By now he had heard enough about Tony Marcus to feel as if he knew him and his two top body men, Junior and Ty Bop.

Before Junior had let him into the office he'd said, 'Gonna need the piece I know you got on you someplace.'

Jesse grinned. 'No,' he said.

'Say what?'

'Say no,' Jesse said. 'Tony wouldn't have told me to come down here if he thought my intent was to shoot him.'

Junior focused a long, dead-eyed look on him, then opened the door. The skinny kid, at least he looked like a kid to Jesse, leaning against the wall inside had to be Ty Bop, whom Sunny said could shoot the numbers off a debit card. He was wearing an oversized old Patriots jersey with Tom Brady's number 12 on it. Old school.

Tony Marcus made no move to get up from behind his desk. He wore a beige summer suit, a blue shirt, a canary-and-blue-striped tie, and a pocket square that matched the canary in the tie. He had a neatly trimmed beard with just a touch of gray in it, same as his hair. If he was dying it, the job was artfully done.

'Heard you done lost your woman,' Marcus said as a way of greeting.

'*Misplaced* might be a better way of putting it,' Jesse said. 'Like when you can't find where you put your car keys.'

'That's only for people got to drive themselves,' Marcus said.

'We're taking a time-out,' Jesse said.

'Boy who'd get himself into a time-out with Miss Sunny Randall shouldn't be allowed to be no chief of police,' Marcus said. 'Poor judgment like that's just another reason why nobody trusts cops no more.'

Tony Marcus looked over at his man Junior, who was as big as Sunny said he was, and said, 'Yo, J. You ever remember a cop thought he could invite his ass in here like this?'

Junior shook his head. Even his head looked as big as a bowling ball.

Marcus turned back to Jesse.

'So you looking for intel on my boy Darnell Woodson?' he said.

'Vinnie says that you retired Darnell from being one of your boys,' Jesse said, 'though not permanently.'

'How is Vinnie, now that you mention him?'

Jesse told him he had a gig going in Vegas.

'Give him my best and tell him to stay the fuck away from me when he gets back,' Marcus said. 'So tell me something: How'd Darnell end up in *your* business.'

'Still not sure he is,' Jesse said. 'But if he is, trying to get out ahead of him. One of my deputies shot Richie Carr last night.'

'Heard about that,' Tony Marcus said. 'Heard your deputy is a girl. Which girl, *Annie Oakley*?'

Jesse shrugged. 'Vinnie said that Darnell and Richie partnered up.'

Marcus lightly tapped his tented fingers underneath his chin. His fingernails gleamed in the soft light of the office.

'Ebony and Ivory,' he said. 'Darnell went off, after he accepted early retirement, and damned if he didn't find himself a mad dog worse than he is.'

'Early retirement,' Jesse said.

'Means I let the boy live,' Marcus said. Then he shook his head and whistled softly. 'Amazing, I get to thinking about it, that either one of them lived long enough *to* get taken out by that girl cop of yours.'

'I'm trying to figure out if he's up in my town,' Jesse said. 'Darnell, I mean. And who he might be working for.'

'If he is in your town, he ain't likely to take his partner getting shot up lightly,' Marcus said.

Jesse asked if Marcus was aware of the land business. He told Jesse that he made it *his* business to know about anything that had that much money around it.

'Why I'm here,' Jesse said, 'is because I was wondering if you might find out who Darnell might be working for.'

Tony Marcus smiled then.

'Are you under the impression that you got some kind

154

of capital with me because you were hitting it with Sunny Randall?' he said. ''Cause if so, it is my duty to disavow you of that notion.'

Tony shook his head and said, 'The stones on you, Chief Jesse Stone.'

'Would it help if she called?' Jesse said, smiling back at him.

'You was gonna ask her to do that, you would've done it already,' Marcus said.

'An innocent young woman got shot in the head,' Jesse said. 'I'm just trying to square up on that.'

'Shee-it,' Tony Marcus said. 'You mean you down here appealing to my better angels? Because I got none.'

'Sunny helped you find out who shot your girlfriend once,' Jesse said.

He saw something change in Tony Marcus's eyes then, without him changing his expression, or moving a muscle. Something dark and subtle at the same time. Jesse had always been told that the eyes were the window to the soul. Maybe that worked if you didn't have a soul.

'Sunny Randall gets to play that card,' he said. 'Not you.'

Jesse said, 'Just asking you to come down on the right side of this, not with jag-offs like Carr and Darnell Woodson.'

They sat there in silence for a moment, as if still taking the measure of each other. But even having been here a few minutes, Jesse knew that Marcus was everything that Sunny had said he was, slick and calculating and charming when he wanted to be, and dangerous as a pipe bomb.

'Maybe I can see what I can see and hear what I can hear,' he said finally. 'And then maybe, if I find out something, I give it to you and maybe I don't.'

He smiled again. There was no mirth or warmth in that smile.

'Now get your cop ass out my office and don't come back,' Tony Marcus said.

Jesse thought about adding, 'Good talk,' but didn't, having

decided that the prudent thing was getting his cop ass out of there.

51

Crow drove over to Marshport and sat outside Blair Richmond's hospital room. He wasn't sure why. He'd spent only a few minutes with the girl. Felt like she was scared of him the whole time he was with her that day.

He'd done plenty of gun work himself in his life, though never once shooting a woman. He'd killed plenty of men. But who put a gun to the head of a kid like this and fired? He knew who. Richie Carr.

But who hired somebody to do shit like that?

Crow was still sitting there when he knew he'd gone past visiting hours. None of the nurses had told him to leave. He scared them, too, he knew. The girl's sister had long since been out of the room. Crow had stayed in the waiting room down the hall until she left. He didn't want to talk to her, tell her how sorry he was, have to explain who he was, why he was here.

He got out of the chair one of the nurses had brought for him and walked to the door and stared through the window at Blair Richmond, who looked like a little girl asleep in her bed, made smaller by the monitors and machines she was attached to.

Stone had asked the question: *What about her had gotten to him this way?*

He had always prided himself on never getting attached or involved, letting his emotions get in the way of things he needed to get done.

Somehow, though, this girl had gotten to him. Now he was like Stone, he had to know who had hired Richie Carr to shoot Blair Richmond and then end up shooting Molly Crane. He knew Molly could take care of herself. Damn, damn, *god*damn, she was tough. What Stone, the old ballplayer, called a tough out.

It was different with this kid. All she'd wanted to do was protect some ocean land. Only nobody had protected her, and maybe her boyfriend, too, from a cockroach like Carr.

Crow turned and walked down the hallway and got into the elevator and got into the rental car and drove back to Paradise and then over the bridge to Stiles Island, one he had helped blow up once without giving it a second thought, and all the way to Billy Singer's rented house.

Maybe Richie Carr was with Billy Singer, too, even though he already had Santo and Baldelli on the payroll. Or maybe Carr was with Barrone. Or Lawton. Still no way to know for sure.

He still hadn't forgotten that somebody had punched Molly Crane in the face.

Crow was suddenly tired of just letting the game come to him and Stone, that was something he was sure about. As he pulled up on the street in front of Singer's house he saw Santo and Baldelli on the front porch, both of them in rocking chairs, either side of the door, feet up on the railing. They both stood up when they saw Crow casually come up the walk and up the steps.

'Relax,' he said. 'Billy's expecting me.'

'I'll go check on that, if it's just the same with you,' Santo said.

Crow had his gun stuffed into the back pocket of his jeans. He took it out and swung it hard across the side of Santo's face, and then again as he was going down. Before Baldelli could clear his gun, Crow turned and pointed his at his face.

'Shhhh,' he said, raising his free hand and putting a finger to his lips.

He told Baldelli to put his gun on the ground. He did. Santo was still conscious, but barely. He was bleeding from the head. Crow motioned Baldelli down the steps as he grabbed Santo by the front of his shirt and dragged him down the steps as they all walked to where the car was parked.

Crow reached into a front pocket and pulled out his key fob and popped the trunk.

'Help him in,' Crow said to Baldelli.

'Fuck you,' Baldelli said.

Crow effortlessly swung the gun and this time caught Baldelli on the side of his head, and now he went down in the street. He lifted Santo into the trunk first, then pulled up Baldelli and shoved him in next.

It was a big enough trunk for both of them, Crow knew, for all the bitching they were both doing. Crow figured he would have to pay extra for the blood on the carpet when he turned it in.

'You gonna just leave us in here?' Santo said. 'I could bleed out.'

'Okay,' Crow said.

Crow went back up the walk and through the front door. That show *Shark Tank* with the guy who owned the Dallas Mavericks was on the flat-screen television. Singer came out of the kitchen with a drink in his hand. Johnnie Walker Blue for him, too, as Crow remembered. When he looked up at Crow, he said, 'What the hell?'

'You need to think about better security, Billy,' Crow said.

Then Crow put his gun away and was across the room and grabbing Singer by the front of his shirt and throwing him up against the wall near the television, the glass falling onto the marble floor and shattering.

'Did you hire Richie Carr?' Crow said, his face close enough to Singer's to smell the scotch on his breath.

'Who's Richie Carr?' Singer said, choking out the words.

Crow pulled him off the wall and then slammed him back into it.

'He's the guy who shot that girl in the head last night,' Crow said. 'And shot Stone's deputy.'

'I swear to God, Crow, I got nothing to do with any of that,' he said. 'Like I had nothing to do with those breakins, whether you believe me or not. Now let me go.'

'After we come to an understanding,' Crow said.

'About what?'

'About how if you call the cops on me after I leave, I'll come back for you even if you've got an army outside,' Crow said. 'Understood?'

'Understood,' Singer said.

He looked very old all of a sudden, Crow thought.

Singer said, 'How come you're not rousting Barrone?'

'You're the only one I know of that brought in some hitters,' Crow said.

'Doesn't mean he didn't, for chrissakes,' Singer said.

He was still struggling for breath.

'Barrone's my next stop,' Crow said.

'Now will you let me go?' Singer said.

Crow grabbed the shirt more firmly, lifting Singer slightly off the ground, getting his face even closer.

'I find out you lied to me and you had something to do with that girl,' Crow said, 'I'll kill you.'

'You got this wrong, Crow, trust me.'

He didn't look desperate to Crow now. Just defeated.

'Something got out of hand here,' Singer said. 'But I swear to God, I've got nothing to do with people dying.'

He let go of him then, watched Singer slide down the wall until he was sitting on the floor. Crow went back outside, collected their guns, tossed them in the front seat of his car. Then he popped the trunk again and told them to get out. They did, cursing him all the way, their faces still covered with blood. Santo said they were going to call the cops. Crow said he might think about checking that with his boss first.

He watched them walk back toward the house, looking over their shoulders at him every few yards. Some nights in Paradise were less boring than others, Crow thought.

52

Jesse asked Suit the next morning where they were with Neil O'Hara's phone records.

'Our district attorney says that nothing has changed,' Suit said. 'Said he's not going to change the rules just because you're still convinced Neil didn't kill himself.'

'It might be easier to convince *him* if I could get my hands on those phone records.'

'You talking to me or to Mr Munroe?' Suit said, grinning.

'Stay on his ass,' Jesse said.

Jesse's door was open. Molly walked through it, as Suit was heading out.

'I thought I told you to take the day,' Jesse said.

'I already took a day.'

'Half.'

'I'm fine,' she said.

'No,' Jesse said, 'you're not, whether you think you are or not.'

Suit went back to his desk. He always said he hated it when Mom and Dad fought.

When Molly sat down Jesse asked if she wanted coffee. She said yes. He made them each a cup with the Keurig, amazed every time he used it how quickly the coffee got made and how good it was. He still would make up a pot from time to time, but now saw that process as taking longer than a ballgame.

'I'd like you to talk to Dix,' Jesse said.

'We already went over this,' she said. 'I don't need a shrink.'

'You got shot, Molls,' Jesse said. 'And when you shot back, the other guy died.'

She stared at him with big and beautiful eyes.

'I went to Mass this morning,' she said. 'The seven o'clock. I prayed for Blair. I even prayed for Richie Carr, acknowledging that it might be too late.'

'What about yourself?'

'I maybe might have thrown in one or two requests for me when the priest asked for special intentions,' she said.

'Have you gotten word to Michael?' Jesse asked.

'I'll tell him all about it when he gets back,' she said. 'And in the telling, which you will back up one hundred percent, I will make the hole in my arm sound about as serious as getting stung by a bee.'

'Good that you floated like a butterfly that night,' Jesse said.

'Shut up,' she said.

'It would be better if you spoke with Dix,' Jesse said. 'I resisted seeing a shrink back in L.A. the first time I put somebody down like you did. Same deal. Kill or be killed. I told them I didn't need to lie down on a couch to deal with it. But afterward I knew it helped.'

'In what way?'

'By convincing me that I had no choice,' Jesse said. 'The difference is, I didn't get shot that time. My partner did. We were running down an alley. After my partner was on the ground, the guy squared up on me. He was a beat too late. I knew I might only get one shot and I took it.'

'I remember the first time you told me about it,' Molly said.

'And I'd do it again,' Jesse said. 'I did it with Crow's old boss Jimmy Macklin back in the day. It was just your turn in the barrel this time. You did good.'

'I don't need to be told that,' she said.

'Good for you to hear, anyway.'

Molly held her mug in both hands and looked at Jesse over it.

'I went over to the hospital last night,' she said. 'I knew it was after visiting hours, but they let me in when I showed them my badge and told them who I was. One of the nurses told me I'd just missed the Native American man, that he'd just been sitting there outside Blair's room.'

She gave a quick shake of her head.

'What is it about her that got to him?' Molly said.

'We might all need Dix, Crow included, to understand that,' Jesse said.

'He's complicated, but we've both always known that.'

'Maybe he really has changed,' Jesse said.

'You think Crow can even remember how many people he's killed?'

'We know how many he's taken out just around here,' Jesse said. 'The guy he was on that getaway boat with. A couple people in the Amber Francisco thing, including Amber's old man.'

'Who'd hired him to find his daughter,' Molly said.

'Hiring him hasn't done Billy Singer much good,' Jesse said. 'Crow's got his own code.'

'A code of getting away with robbery and murder, if you ask me.'

Jesse shrugged. 'When you're good, you're good.'

'Or bad,' Molly said.

She had finished her coffee. She extended the mug toward Jesse and said, 'You want me to rinse this?'

'I got it,' he said.

She said she might take another run over to the hospital to look in on Blair, if that was all right. Jesse told her that of course it was all right. In his mind, she was taking a day. She said she'd let him know when she needed a damn day.

'Yes, sir,' he said.

'Don't give me that,' Molly said.

He was still at his desk when she called an hour later. Jesse asked if she was on her way back. Molly said she was still at the hospital, in Blair's room. It was why she was keeping her voice low.

'You know that guy Darnell Woodson we've been talking about? Richie Carr's partner?' she said. 'I went into the system and pulled up an old mug shot.'

Jesse waited.

'I think I just saw him in the parking lot,' Molly said.

53

Jesse told Molly to stay inside the hospital until he and Suit got there.

'If it's the guy,' she said, 'he's not going to try something in broad daylight.'

'Humor me,' Jesse said.

Suit made a sweep of the visitors' parking lot once they got there, writing down license plate numbers as he did. Jesse went upstairs to Blair's floor, where he met Molly in the lounge up there.

'First things first,' Jesse said. 'How is she?'

'The same,' she said. 'I talked to one of the doctors. He said it's a good thing, this is the best way for her brain to heal. If it's going to heal.'

When they were back in the lobby Jesse said, 'You sure it was him?'

'Her room is only on the third floor,' Molly said. 'He was standing next to my car, almost like he wanted me to see him.'

Jesse said they'd check it before they'd dust it with the kit in his car, to see if he'd put some kind of tracking device on it.

'Most likely he just wants you to know he's here,' Jesse said.

'I shot his partner,' Molly said.

'We don't know for sure that he was partnered up with Carr on this thing, though,' Jesse said. 'But even if he is, or was, it seems like they've closed the loop on anybody who might have been a threat to the land deal. Two are dead and one's upstairs in that room.'

'But still alive,' Molly said.

'Maybe she was the last loose end,' Jesse said.

They were in the parking lot now with Suit. Jesse got his fingerprint kit out of the back of the Explorer and told him to dust Molly's Cherokee with it. Jesse checked the car himself for any kind of bug, but couldn't find one. Then he called the chief in Marshport, Captain Mike Pearl, somebody he'd worked with in the past. He asked Pearl if he could put somebody outside Blair Richmond's room for at least a few days, explaining why. Pearl said he would.

Before Captain Mike Pearl had gotten off the call, he'd told Jesse, 'Holler if you need any help with that hot mess you got going on over there.'

Jesse told him he was considering the Marines at this point.

54

It was early in Los Angeles and Jesse knew that his son had adjusted his schedule of law school classes so that he could sleep in a few days a week. Sometimes he slept at his girlfriend's house, also a law student. Not today. Jesse still had what he thought of as his find-my-kid app on his phone, even on the other side of the country.

He used to have the same thing with Sunny, before she made him disable it.

Jesse knew he should have felt at least somewhat guilty about waking up his son. Even though he had come to fatherhood this late in his life, he was pretty sure rousting your kids out of bed was one of the perks that came with being a parent.

'You in a hostage situation?' Cole mumbled. 'If you are, tell them I'll pay the ransom after I get a couple more hours of sleep.'

'I need a favor,' Jesse said.

'I need a couple more hours of sleep.'

'I'm serious.'

'You never ask me for favors,' Cole said.

He sounded a bit more alert now.

'It's why I feel I have a strong position with you this morning despite waking you up,' Jesse said.

'I am now up in a sitting position,' Cole said. 'What's the favor?'

'I'd like you to do some financial sleuthing for me in your spare time.'

'This was supposed to be my spare time!' Cole shouted.

'It may take some grunt work, but will play nicely into your current area of legal expertise.'

'Expertise?'

'I've seen your grades.'

'So tell me what you need,' Cole said, 'now that I can see my afternoon at Venice Beach with Kim actually disappearing into the ocean.'

Jesse caught him up on what had been happening in Paradise as succinctly as he could. Cole knew some of it, admitted he had no idea things had gotten this bad, this quickly.

'Tell me about it,' Jesse said.

'Why don't you ask that old flame of yours, the one with the flaming red hair and that killer bod?'

They both knew he was referring to Rita Fiore of Cone, Oakes, the top litigator at the biggest and best law firm in Boston.

'I'm out of favors with Rita,' Jesse said, 'at least not the kind I'm looking for here. And if she finds out I'm not with Sunny, provided she doesn't know already, I might find myself being stalked.'

'You dog,' Cole said.

'So can you throw an old one a bone?' Jesse said, and then told him exactly what he needed. He should have asked Cole to do this a week ago, or more, but better late than never.

'How's that girl?' Cole said.

'Hanging in there.'

'You'll figure this all out, Pop,' Cole said.

'How do *you* figure?' Jesse said.

'Because you always do,' Cole said.

Then he said, 'Going back to sleep now.'

'Copy that,' Jesse said.

55

The big house, which looked to Jesse as if the pilgrims might have built it, overlooked the water at Paradise Neck, which had once been the fanciest part of town but was no longer, especially now that beach erosion in this area was getting people to think that some of the older homes over there might eventually slide right into the Atlantic and float away.

The driveway leading up to the house was at least a half-mile long. On the way up, Jesse passed a gatehouse bigger than any house Jesse had ever lived in as a kid. Sometimes Jesse thought that there were really just two kinds of rich in Paradise: old money and older.

Jesse pulled the Explorer into the circular driveway in front of the main house. He hadn't called to say he was coming, feeling as if the worst thing that could happen was him wasting maybe half an hour on the round trip from the station. But there was a Mercedes SUV parked in front of the garage, a lot of lights on inside.

I'm a patient man until I'm not, Jesse had told Dix one time.

'And what happens when you run out of patience?' Dix said.

'Nothing good.'

'At least you don't take a drink anymore when you reach that point.'

'Not today,' Jesse had said to him.

A floodlight had lit the driveway as soon as Jesse pulled up. It was past ten o'clock by now. Jesse knew what Cole had come up with on Lawton could wait until morning. But this was what happened when he got impatient. On top of that, he didn't like getting jacked around by old money.

Or older.

Thomas Lawton opened the door before Jesse was halfway up the cobblestone walk. He was wearing a black T-shirt and baggy tennis shorts that came down to his knees, covering half his skinny legs. He was barefoot.

'What are you doing here?' he said.

'We need to talk, Thomas,' Jesse said.

'What about?'

'You lying to me,' Jesse said.

56

Lawton walked him through the house to the back deck, turning on lights when they got there. They both sat in Adirondack chairs that even Jesse, not an avid consumer, knew were not cheap.

'Now, exactly what is it that I'm supposed to have lied to you about?' Lawton said. 'And so you know, I don't have a lot of time. I've got a date coming over in about half an hour, and I'm guessing it would be kind of a mood killer to have the chief of police on the premises when she arrives.'

Jesse smiled.

'You told me you were rich as shit, Thomas,' he said, 'when it turns out you're pretty much the opposite of that, at least until you sell the land.'

Lawton said, 'You're the one who's *full* of shit.'

'Thinking no,' Jesse said. 'And this is on me, by the way. I did the background work on Billy Singer and money problems that might chase him all the way into jail. And I did the work on Barrone, who still wants people to think he can lick any man in the house, but might be about to sell off one of his casinos, or both of them, if the banks don't take them first. So I knew why they need this deal to go through, and the sooner the better.'

'Is there a point to this fascinating presentation?' Lawton said.

'Once you inherited everything from your old man,' Jesse said, 'you didn't want to make money the boring, old-fashioned way. You wanted to open a club in Boston, which you did. Until you closed it last year. You wanted to open restaurants, and buy racehorses, and even get into show business. But the horses ended up either back in the pack or lame. When you wanted to go Hollywood, you burned money on a couple of big box-office losers, right out of the box. I don't know about you, but I'm detecting a bit of a downward spiral here.'

'Who came up with this?' Lawton said.

'Guy I know who specializes in financial bullshit artists like you,' Jesse said. 'See, I was like everybody else in town when I looked at Trust Fund Thomas. Who came from a long line of Lawtons, most of whom had the best interest of the town at heart.'

'I always assumed that there was something written down saying I couldn't sell it,' Lawton said. 'We went over this already. Turns out there wasn't anything written down.'

'And aren't you the lucky boy because of that,' Jesse said.

'You've got this all wrong,' Lawton said.

'People keep telling me that,' Jesse said. 'About almost everything. I'm starting to doubt myself.'

'And I'm telling you that nobody's ever going to run a benefit for me,' Lawton said. 'I mean, wake up, do you have any idea how much this property we're on right here is worth?'

'No clue,' Jesse said. 'But what I do know now is that you've quietly had it on the market for over a year. And yet here you are.'

'I don't even live here full-time,' he said. 'I spend most of the week at my place in Boston, near where my club used to be.'

Lawton stood up, walked over to the railing, leaned against it, the water behind him in the night.

'Once this deal goes through, I am rich as shit all over again.'

'But if it goes sideways,' Jesse said, 'you're screwed sideways.'

Cole was a law student, not a forensic accountant. But the kid had done good.

'It sounds like you did burn through an awful lot of money in an awfully short time,' Jesse said.

'You have all the fun I've had,' Lawton said, 'eventually you have to pay some dues.'

'Somebody is killing people over this land,' Jesse said. 'I'm going to find out who it is.'

Lawton came back across the deck and sat down, then leaned forward in his chair.

'For the last time,' he said, 'you've got me all wrong. Did I get hurt with some bad investments and some truly shitty judgments? Guilty. But if you think that I've had people killed this close to cashing out, you're nuts.'

'Unless the people who got killed were in the way.'

'They weren't.'

'Any chance I'm going to find a connection between you and an ex-cop named Richie Carr?' Jesse said.

'The guy I read shot your deputy and the tree hugger?' Lawton said. 'No.'

'Blair,' Jesse said.

'Excuse me?'

'The tree hugger. Her name is Blair. And if you call her a

tree hugger again I am going to come over there and stick your elbow in your ear.'

'Sorry,' Lawton said.

Jesse said, 'You ever hear of a guy named Darnell Woodson?'

'Who's that?'

'Richie Carr's partner. If I do some digging, any chance I might find a connection between *him* and you?'

'Knock yourself out, because I never heard of the guy,' he said. 'But you'll probably have as much luck with that digging as those kids did digging those graves on my land.'

Jesse got up and walked over to Lawton, close enough that Lawton couldn't have gotten up if he wanted to. So Jesse was looking straight down at him. A cop thing.

'You still lying to me, Thomas?' Jesse said.

'I'm just trying to get out of the way and let this happen now,' Lawton said.

Jesse stood there for a moment longer. Lawton continued to stare up at him. There was just a hint of fear in his eyes, as if he was afraid Jesse might suddenly slap him.

'Those kids couldn't stop this deal from going through,' Lawton said. 'Neil wouldn't have been able to stop it if he lived.'

'Maybe I still can,' Jesse said.

'I thought you told Gary Armistead and me that wasn't your job,' Lawton said.

'*I* lied,' Jesse said.

57

'Admit you were surprised when you opened the door,' Molly said to Crow.

They were in the small kitchen of his Airbnb. He'd made

coffee for them and then poured a little whiskey out of his flask and into the mugs before he brought them to the table.

'I got that doorbell cam thing on my phone,' Crow said. 'The way I set it up, the range extends to the street. So I saw you pull up. My world, you don't much like surprises.'

Molly saw him almost smile then. Almost, but not quite.

'But there are exceptions to every rule,' he said.

She sipped some coffee. The whiskey made it go down much easier.

Moth to a flame, she thought.

'I just wanted to thank you,' she said, 'for being concerned about Blair.'

'Not that it's helping her very much.'

'Still,' Molly said.

'That the only reason you came?' Crow said.

'Sorry,' Molly said. And shrugged. 'All I got.'

'I'm not sorry,' Crow said.

They both knew what he meant.

'Well, I am,' Molly said.

She had taken a shower and fixed her hair and her face and put on one of her favorite shirts and her favorite pair of white jeans, Seven brand, a gift from Sunny Randall.

'I never should have let it happen,' Molly said.

'We both *let* it happen,' Crow said. 'And we both know that, by then, there was no stopping it.'

'There's always a way to stop it,' Molly said. 'I could have said no.'

'No to me or no to yourself?'

He poured a little more whiskey into his mug. He offered it to Molly. She shook her head.

'I should have said no to it, to us, to everything,' she said. 'But that's in the past, where it belongs.' She absently rubbed her arm where she'd been shot. 'I just finally came to the conclusion that I needed to stop blaming you. Being mean to you. Jesse's right. I'm mostly angry at myself.'

171

Crow stared at her. Again, he almost smiled.

'You read Hemingway?' he said.

Didn't see that coming.

Molly told him she assumed just about everybody had read at least one Hemingway book.

'I'm not a big reader,' Crow said. 'But I read just about everything he ever wrote. And one time he wrote that what's moral is what feels good after. That's the part most people quote. But he followed the line up by saying that what's immoral is what makes you feel bad after.'

'I remember both lines,' Molly said.

'So which one is it with you?' he said. 'If we're speaking about us.'

'There is no us,' Molly said, 'other than the "us" working this case together.'

'But there was.'

'For one night,' she said. 'The one night when I cheated on a man I've loved pretty much my whole life. I don't cheat on anything, Wilson. I tell the kid at the checkout counter if they somehow undercharged me at the grocery store. If the government sends too much money after we file our taxes, I calculate the difference and send it back. *That's* me. Not that night.'

She drank the last of her coffee.

'With me, the immoral beats the moral that Hemingway wrote about all day long,' Molly said.

Now Crow smiled.

'We could do it again,' he said, 'just to make sure.'

'Could,' she said. 'But can't. And won't.'

'But not because you don't want to.'

'I didn't come here to have this conversation,' Molly said to him.

'We seem to be having it anyway,' Crow said.

She wanted to do something, right now, to change the energy in the room. Now that they were working together, she had started to wonder all over again what it would be like to be alone with him, to be this close to him. *No,* she thought. That wasn't right. She knew exactly what it would be like. Coming here had just confirmed it.

'What I want,' she said finally, her voice sounding thick, 'is to go home and check in with the hospital one last time on Blair and then get into bed.'

'You could do that here.'

'No,' Molly said. Now she smiled. 'There. I said it.'

'Can I at least walk you to your car?' Crow said.

'No,' Molly said again.

Saying it was actually easy, once you got the hang of it.

58

Mayor Gary Armistead announced on Friday morning that he had moved up the Board of Selectmen's vote, which he said would now take place the following Wednesday.

'Surprised he didn't just go ahead and get the thing passed in the middle of the night,' Jesse said.

'You still think that he might end up with a piece of this deal when this is all over?' Molly said.

'I've had this feeling all along that our Gary already knows who's going to walk away with the land,' Jesse said. 'That the whole thing about sealed bids is bullshit. So maybe it's not him looking for a piece of the action as much as leverage with the winner. Politicians love people, especially rich people, who owe them favors.'

She said she was going back to the hospital. She went over at least once a day. This was the best time for her to do it. A few minutes later Suitcase Simpson came in with Neil's tox screen, the one Dev Chadha had sent over. The one that said oxycodone had been in Neil's system when he died.

Jesse called Dev.

'Pain pills?' he said. 'Really?'

'Or he ingested it without knowing because somebody wanted to knock him out,' Dev said. 'Oxy is a pretty potent knockout drug if somebody wants to use it that way.'

'He had enough of it in him to knock him out?' Jesse asked.

'Hell, yes,' Dev said.

'Did Neil have a prescription for the stuff?'

'Gene Bednarik was Neil's doctor,' Dev said. 'He's a friend. I called him when I got the results back and asked if Neil was in some kind of pain that might have required oxy. He said not once in the twenty years he'd been treating him.' Dev paused. 'And by the way, Chief? Neil also had some wine in his system, too. Even if he had popped one of those pills, he couldn't have been enough of a dumbass to wash it down with alcohol.'

'So he could have been unconscious when he died,' Jesse said.

'It's the way I'd bet,' he said.

There was a silence then, until Dev said, 'Why did somebody want it to look like a suicide with Neil?'

'Maybe to throw me off and buy some time,' Jesse said. 'Like one of those misdirection plays they talk about in football. Keep me off balance. Or looking over there, when I needed to be looking somewhere else. Basically keep me from getting up into their shit for as long as possible, at least until the deal went down.'

He ended the call. Sat with Dev's paperwork on the desk in front of him.

Richie Carr was an ex-cop. Could he have tried to stage a suicide, and put his hands on oxy, and beaten Ben Gage before he shot him? No reason why he couldn't have done all of those things. If it was Carr, he'd done a pretty good job making it look as if Neil had shot himself. Just not good enough.

He's not as good a cop as I am.

Sunny sometimes talked about the 'MacGuffin' when she

was working a case of her own. She said it was the thing in Hitchcock movies that drove the story. An object sometimes. An event. Even a piece of paper. Something that motivated the characters, and kept raising the stakes.

What was it here?

Suit came back into Jesse's office just as Jesse was about to head over to Daisy Dyke's and pick up sandwiches for him and Suit and Molly, since it was his turn.

'I found kind of an interesting phone call Neil made on his landline,' Suit said. 'The day he died.'

'I thought we couldn't get the records on the landline, either,' Jesse said, 'thanks to our hardo district attorney.'

Suit smiled.

'We couldn't,' he said. 'But here's the thing: I went over to talk to Neil's old assistant. Lauren Potter? I went out with her in high school.'

'Of course you did,' Jesse said.

'Anyway, Lauren went to the ladies' room while I was there,' Suit said. 'And I looked on her desk and happened to see mail addressed to Neil, from last month. His phone bill was in the stack.'

'And you took it.'

'Without hesitation,' Suit said. 'I think he must have used his cell phone more. Because there weren't all that many outgoing calls from his desk phone over the past month.'

'Neil never treated any kind of phone as a pacifier,' Jesse said. 'He liked to conduct business face-to-face, as often as he could.'

'On his last day,' Suit continued, 'he made one call to the Gull. Another was to his wife, or ex-wife, or whatever we're calling her.'

'That lines up,' Jesse said. 'She told me he asked her out to dinner. Told me how badly she felt that she turned him down.'

'But it turns out there was one call that wasn't local,' Suit said. 'That was the interesting one.'

'And you checked out the number,' Jesse said.

'I did.'

Then Suit told him who the recipient was.

'No shit,' Jesse said.

'None,' Suit said.

Jesse was already getting the keys to the Explorer out of the top drawer of his desk.

'You know what a MacGuffin is?' Jesse asked him.

'Only if it's like a McMuffin,' Suit said.

By then Jesse was already out the door, calling Crow on his way to the parking lot, asking if he wanted to make a quick road trip, that his heritage might turn out to be useful for once.

59

The offices of the Peccontac Tribal Nation, next door to its museum, were in Clifton, Mass, a little under an hour from Paradise. Jesse had called the number Suit had given him, gotten no answer, and decided to drive over with Crow from Paradise anyway.

The tribal leader, Terry Harvey, was in his own office when he got there, looking as if he'd just moved in, boxes stacked against the walls. He explained that the building they were in, home to the sovereign government of the Peccontac people and its various branches and programs, had undergone a massive and long-overdue renovation, and that he'd gone on vacation to get away for a few weeks while the job was finally completed.

When he'd introduced himself and given his title, Harvey had smiled at Jesse's obvious surprise. He was in his mid-thirties, Jesse guessed, maybe younger, and looked more like a preppie than someone with his title and responsibilities.

'You were perhaps expecting a headdress and war paint?' Harvey said.

'I hope I'm more evolved than that with cultural assessments,' Jesse said.

'I'm trying to bring him along,' Crow said. 'Slow process.'

Harvey explained that he'd attended Harvard and Harvard Law, joining the biggest law firm in Boston after graduating from the law school.

'Cone, Oakes,' Harvey said. 'You've heard of it?'

Jesse said that, as a matter-of-fact, he had.

'They came at me pretty hard. I was Harvard, I was Native American, I checked a lot of boxes for them.'

'You know Rita Fiore?' Jesse said.

'Doesn't every lawyer in town know her?' Harvey said. 'I actually worked on a couple cases for her.'

Terry Harvey told them he'd finally decided he wanted to do more with his life than practice law after his father, the tribal leader before him, had died. He came home to Clifton and made it his mission to give Peccontac Nation an even greater sense of community and pride and shared history. Their museum, he said, fully funded by their government, was one of the best of its kind for any tribe in North America, and his personal pride and joy.

He wore a button-down shirt, a sleeveless sweater vest, khaki pants. Jesse thought he actually looked more like the leader of Vineyard Vines.

Harvey nodded at Crow.

'Who are your people?' he said.

'Apache,' Crow said.

'Which tribe?'

'Kiowa,' Crow said.

Jesse knew Crow was bluffing. The one time Jesse had pressed him on the tribe of his ancestors, Crow had said Jicarilla. Molly said he'd told her Mescalero. Neither one of them had been sure he was even Apache.

'We don't run into a lot of Apaches in this part of the country,' Harvey said.

'You should be fine with him if you don't make any sudden moves,' Jesse said.

'I've actually been expecting someone from your town to reach back out to me,' he said.

'Back out?' Jesse said.

'I was just clearing my messages,' he said. He grinned rather sheepishly. 'My wife made me promise no business while we were away. The very last message before the tape cut off turned out to be from your mayor.'

'You know he's since died,' Jesse said.

'I read that,' Harvey said. 'I actually tried to call up his replacement before you showed up, but forgot it was Saturday.'

Jesse asked if he could hear the message. Harvey reached over to his phone setup and pushed PLAY.

'Mr Harvey,' he said, 'this is Mayor O'Hara calling from Paradise. In a bit of a rush right now, and you're probably gone for the day. But I would like to take a ride over tomorrow and ask you some questions about tribal history, and some property up here. There may be some question...' That was where the message ended.

'This is about the land being sold in Paradise, is it not?' Harvey said. 'Do you think Mr O'Hara was suggesting the land might belong to us?'

Jesse sat there, processing the possibilities.

'My people have an expression that might cover this,' he said. 'Fuckin' ay.'

There was a huge map on the wall behind him.

'The Peccontac people have literally been around Massachusetts for thousands of years,' Terry Harvey continued. 'More in the Marshport and Oxbow area, and up the coast north of Paradise, or so I thought.' He hooked a thumb at the map behind him. 'New maps, even from the olden days, are constantly turning up. We were mostly comprised of agrarian and fishing communities, all the way into the 1800s. And spoiler alert? We have always been of the belief that the government stole land from us and began selling it to the white founders of those towns. We've just never had enough proof on that particular area. Some of our tribal leaders tried to challenge a big chunk of property in Oxbow after the First World War. Where that state park is now.'

Near where Molly had found Blair Richmond.

'But the case went nowhere.' Harvey continued. 'Again, because of lack of proof. I frankly wasn't following what was going on in Paradise all that closely, because I've never seen any credible documentation about the land there. But that doesn't mean it doesn't belong to us.'

He sighed.

'This goes on all the time, of course, all around the country,' he said. 'Most of the times, when our side has won, it turns out that there was no federal sign-off on land like this. And when tribes have been able to prove it, they've been able to prove that nobody can sell it, because it still *belongs* to this tribe or that. At the very least, if there is authentic proof, it becomes a fate worse than death for the person trying to sell the land and the one trying to buy it, because of a thing called "clouded title."'

'But it sounds like Neil might have been suggesting that basically your people might have gotten to the property being sold first.'

'Fuckin' ay,' Terry Harvey said. 'Back in the day we didn't have the kind of political power that we have now.'

'What proof do you think Neil might have had?' Jesse said.

It had been jarring, and more than somewhat, hearing Neil's voice again.

'It could be any number of things, easily verifiable by experts,' Harvey said. 'Something as simple as a title, or treaty, no one knew existed. It was the Europeans who started the title system. To show you have a good one, you follow a chain all the way back to an original owner. Maybe he found the kind of artifacts that were often buried with children, if it *is* a burial site. Religious objects. Skeletal remains would be best. There's a laundry list of things that could throw into question that whoever claims ownership to the land now never did acquire it legally in the first place from our tribe. If we felt as if we had real evidence, and as crazy as this sounds, we could invoke something called the Nonintercourse Act from the late *1700*s, and challenge the fact that the approval from the federal government was never given in the first place. But this sort of litigation, all across the country, has often turned out to be a bear.'

He paused. 'And without getting further into the weeds, there was a case not long ago where three tribes of Oneida Indians brought suit for damages and won for land that had been conveyed right before the turn of the nineteenth century.'

'But if the proof exists, and it does turn out to be authentic…?' Jesse said, his voice trailing off.

'Do you have the proof in your possession?' Harvey said.

'Not yet,' Jesse said.

And maybe not ever.

'Well, if and when you do, I would very much like to see it,' he said. 'So would our lawyers.'

'Not as much as I want to see it,' Jesse said.

'Once I heard the message today, I read back a little more on what's happening in Paradise,' he said. 'Seems to be the whole process of that land being sold to one of those two developers is pretty much a foregone conclusion. Isn't the vote in a few days?'

'It is,' Jesse said. 'But there was an old Yankee who said, "It ain't over 'til it's over."'

'Yogi,' Terry Harvey said. 'Even Red Sox fans know that one.'

'This deal has gotten two people killed so far,' Jesse said. 'And nearly a third.'

'So maybe the land really doesn't belong to this Thomas Lawton?' Harvey said.

'And maybe never did,' Crow said. 'Maybe his family engaged in old white-man custom known as stealing.'

'Tell me how I can help,' Harvey said. 'We're obviously very invested now.'

'Keep this between us for now,' Jesse said.

Harvey grinned at them and held up his right hand, palm facing Jesse and Crow. 'You have my solemn word.'

'Say we do find proof,' Jesse said. 'What happens then?'

'At the very least,' Terry Harvey said, 'we slap an injunction on this guy Lawton, and the whole thing ends up in federal court, perhaps for a very long time.'

'But Lawton, if we find what we need to find in time, would have no legal standing on selling the land?' Jesse said.

'Not unless he wants to pick a fight with a tribe a lot more dangerous than mine is,' Harvey said.

'Which one?' Crow said.

'My old law firm,' the leader of the Peccontac Nation said. 'The tribe known as Cone, Oakes.'

60

When they were back in Paradise, Crow said he was going over to the hospital. Jesse told him that he'd instructed the nurses and doctors to call him if there was any change in her condition.

'So if there's a change, I'll make the call instead,' Crow said.

Suit was at his desk when Jesse walked in. He said he was still waiting on the subpoena that would allow them to search Richie Carr's Land Cruiser. For now it sat in the big lot for impounded cars in Marshport that Mike Pearl let the PPD use sometimes, waiting for the red tape to part, somewhat like the

Red Sea. Suit said that at least he'd gotten no sense that Ellis Munroe was going to slow-walk them on this one.

Jesse occasionally thought that red tape like this was a form of domestic terrorism.

Before Suit left for the day, Jesse told him what he and Crow had learned in Clifton.

'This is a big deal, right?' Suit said.

'Not without proof it's not,' Jesse said. 'And do not mention this to anyone, including Elena.'

Suit thumbs-upped him.

'You just need to find the thing,' Suit said. 'Or things.'

Jesse said it sounded a lot simpler when you put it that way.

He had already begun to feel an interior ticking clock as he drove home from the station. Maybe he could stop the deal even after Ed Barrone or Billy Singer ended up with the winning bid. But he knew the best way to stop it was before the vote.

Find the MacGuffin.

Did Neil hide it? Did Ben Gage hide it?

And hiding it from whom?

No one had beaten Neil O'Hara before he was shot. But it appeared they'd drugged him. Somebody *had* beaten Ben Gage. The same person, or persons? Somebody wanted Neil's death to look like a suicide. But not Ben Gage's. He'd either told them what they wanted to know, or not. He was going to end up dead either way.

Goddamn, I could use a drink.

The urge still came up on Jesse that quickly. That easily. In the old days, that was how it started. Quickly, easily. He got out of his chair and drove over to Marshport for the six o'clock AA meeting. He hadn't been in a while. But then the wolf hadn't been back at the door lately.

The speaker was a Catholic priest who'd spent the last six months in rehab. Six months. Jesse thought it might be some kind of world's record, at least from the stories he'd ever heard in these rooms, or when he was in rehab himself. Insurance paid for only twenty-eight days. Those companies didn't have the kind of money the Catholic Church did.

Jesse didn't stay around for coffee. He drove back home and turned on the Sox game and thought about calling Sunny. Even took out his phone and was about to speed-dial her. But then put the phone down as quickly as he'd pulled it out. Watched the game until it slogged its way into the fifth inning and went to bed early.

Somebody was lying to him. Maybe more than one of them was lying. Or all of them were. And him an officer of the law. The town really was going to hell.

61

Jesse and Molly and Suit were in the conference room. The subpoena on Richie Carr's SUV had been approved by the judge, so Jesse had sent Gabe Weathers over to Marshport to search it, including the car's navigation system.

'Am I looking for anything in particular?' Gabe had said.

'Anything and everything,' Jesse said.

'Oh, good,' Gabe said. 'That narrows things down considerably.'

'Come back with something I can use or you're fired,' Jesse said.

'Wish I had a dollar for every time I heard that one,' Gabe said.

'We all do,' Molly said.

Jesse had been explaining to Molly and Suit that he couldn't come up with a single good reason for going to Gary Armistead with what he'd learned from Terry Harvey, the message Neil had left for him, the implications of it for Lawton and Singer and Barrone and Harvey and the town.

'Gary would want to see some proof, too,' Jesse said.

'Which we don't have,' Suit said.

'Yet,' Jesse said.

'Roger that,' Suit said.

'How about this?' Molly said, brightening. 'How about we leak it to Nellie Shofner that the ownership of the land might be in question, and have her write that up for the *Crier*.'

'Thought of that,' Jesse said.

'Did not,' she said.

'Here we go,' Suit said.

'For now, putting it out there doesn't get me to where I want to go,' Jesse said. 'It also brings the tribe into it for no good reason. And maybe has Armistead fast-track the process even more.'

Jesse had brought donuts. Suit ate another one. Molly gave him a look. He said he was just trying to be polite.

'Say we do find proof,' Suit said. 'What happens next?'

'I'm no lawyer...' Jesse said.

'Though you have slept with a few,' Molly said.

'... but I did do some reading,' Jesse continued. 'And it confirmed what Terry Harvey told me. They would slap a temporary restraining order on Lawton, and drop-kick the whole thing to federal court like champions.'

'Once it gets there,' Molly said, 'the deal is as good as dead.'

'And two people are dead for nothing,' Jesse said.

Molly said, 'Another one is fighting for her life.'

Jesse pointed to the last donut and told Suit to go for it.

'I'm missing something here,' Jesse said. 'I know it.'

'You never miss anything,' Molly said.

'Always a first time,' he said.

He thought about going over to Marshport and helping Gabe search the car. He told Molly and Suit that he was going to make one last pass through Neil O'Hara's house instead. He was sitting behind Neil's desk when he heard the front door open. He kept his hand on his gun as he walked into the hallway and saw Kate O'Hara standing there.

62

'They told me when I stopped by the station that you were here,' she said.

'What were you doing at the station?' Jesse said.

'I wanted to stop by and say goodbye,' she said.

'Where are you going?'

'I'm going to be leaving soon,' she said. 'Thought I might start in Paris. It's time to be somewhere besides Paradise. And perhaps be someone else.' She smiled. 'Such an odd name for a town, isn't it? Especially when it's so often the opposite of that.'

Jesse walked back into Neil's den. Kate followed him.

'I guess this is a way for me to say goodbye to Neil, too,' she said.

'Have you found what you're looking for in here?' she said to Jesse.

'Nothing even remotely resembling a clue,' Jesse said.

'Good old Jesse,' she said. 'Still a dog with a bone.'

'Keeps me out of trouble,' he said.

She smiled again.

'I was under the impression, Chief, that you frequently go looking for trouble.'

Her eyes seemed to take in the whole room at once.

'My husband the hoarder,' she said. 'He had a room like this at our house. I still walk in sometimes, even though he cleaned it out, and feel as if the stuff is still here.'

'What's going to happen to all of it?' he said. 'His stuff?'

'I'll eventually put the house up for sale,' she said. 'I was going to have everything packed into some boxes and put in storage.

His only living relative is a half-sister who lives in Hawaii. She's still afraid to fly, even after COVID-19. She can keep what she wants, I suppose, if she ever makes it back.

'What specifically were those people looking for when they broke in here?' she said. 'And when they broke into my house?'

'Beats me,' Jesse said.

She smiled at him again. It was a sad smile, in a room filled as much with sadness as Neil's belongings, but somehow still dazzling, at least to him.

'There aren't many things I'm going to miss in this town,' Kate said. 'But you're one of them, Jesse.'

'You know the drill,' he said. 'Right place, wrong time. Happens to the best of us.'

'Do you ever wonder how things could have worked out differently?'

'All the time,' he said.

It was a lie, he knew, but one that cost him nothing.

She stepped forward now and kissed him lightly on the lips, then put a hand to his cheek.

'I hope you find what you're looking for, Kate,' Jesse said.

Another smile.

'I was about to say the same thing to you,' she said.

She left him standing there in her late husband's den. *Another one that got away*, Jesse thought. By now there were enough of them to form a conga line.

63

'Talk to me,' Dix said to Jesse.

Dix had always told Jesse that if he ever needed him on a weekend, all he needed to do was call. So they were in Dix's office on Sunday morning.

Dix looked as he always did, backlit by the sun slashing through the partially closed blinds behind him, bald head gleaming, white shirt looking dry-cleaner crisp, hands perfectly manicured even though Dix had once admitted he tended to his nails himself, desk so neat it looked as if he were expecting some kind of inspection. Somehow almost completely still, but completely alert at the same time.

Jesse had never been able to picture him as the drunk cop Dix had once been.

'It's not personal today,' Jesse said. 'What I'm here for.'

'Thanks for the heads-up,' Dix said.

'I mean,' Jesse said, 'I have an unresolved situation with Sunny. But nothing has changed with resolving it since the last time I was here.'

'Or the time before that,' Dix said. 'Is she still in Los Angeles?'

'Yes.'

'Want to talk about that?'

'I don't,' Jesse said. 'It's actually not making me crazy.'

'Stop using those complicated clinical expressions,' Dix said. 'And stop self-diagnosing.'

'It's the case that's making me crazy,' Jesse said.

'Talk to me,' Dix said again.

Jesse took him through it. He'd actually brought notes, the timeline he'd worked out, so he didn't leave anything out. Dix called it a cheat sheet.

'I may have left some things out,' Jesse said.

Dix smiled. 'Somehow I doubt that.'

'I'd like you to look at it like a cop,' Jesse said.

'It'll be a stretch.' Dix smiled again.

Then he said, 'You know the professional *is* always personal with you, right?'

'Maybe more personal this time because of Neil and those two kids,' Jesse said.

'You couldn't save him,' Dix said. 'But I get the sense that you feel as if there were more you could have done to save the kids. The young woman in the hospital especially.'

'More than somewhat,' Jesse said.

Dix leaned back in his chair, clasping his fingers behind his head, staring up at the ceiling fan above them. When he leaned forward again he said, 'I think you might be looking at this wrong.'

'Tell me how.'

Dix said, 'I'm thinking, just listening to the way you laid it out, that maybe Neil didn't die for what he *had*, necessarily. It may have been because of what he knew that night. The proof itself, in that moment, seems secondary to me, whether he actually had it in his possession or Ben Gage did.'

Jesse waited.

Dix said, 'I think whoever killed him, and then killed the young man, just wanted to close the circle as quickly as they could, and then figure out finding the relics or whatever the hell it is they were looking for, afterward.'

'You're saying somebody panicked,' Jesse said.

'It's the only thing that makes sense to me,' Dix said. 'Somebody found out what Neil knew, and what the kid had, and killed them both.'

'I still don't know where Neil went after he called the museum that day,' Jesse said.

Dix smiled brilliantly now.

'We still talking cop to cop?' he said.

'Always,' Jesse said.

'Find out, for fuck's sake.'

64

Stone was right, Crow thought.

They were missing something.

Crow grinned at himself in his rearview mirror.

Look at me, he thought. *Trying to think like a cop.*

But if they weren't missing something, they would have tamped this thing down solid a long time ago and he would be on his way out of town now.

Where to? He hadn't played that out in his head yet. He wasn't going back to Vegas; he knew that Billy Singer might put a bounty on him if he didn't get the land. Crow just knew he couldn't stay here. And knew why, too. He didn't want to be close to her, start imagining a life with her he could never have, even thinking about it for one minute made him feel like a fool.

One thing for sure.

She could still get under his skin.

The girl lying in that hospital bed had gotten under his skin, too.

He hadn't seen that coming.

It seemed like ten years ago that he had showed up here working for Billy. He was thinking about Billy a lot tonight. He'd actually believed Billy the night he'd scared the shit out of him after putting Santo and Baldelli in the trunk. When Billy said he didn't know anything about Richie Carr shooting the girl and Molly. Just because Billy knew the consequences of lying to Crow.

It had to mean that Carr, and maybe his partner, had hired out to either Barrone or Lawton.

No other players in the game, at least that Jesse and Crow knew about.

Seller or buyer?

189

Both of them, and Billy, too, geeked out to get this thing done. Were Barrone and Lawton more desperate than Billy? Who the hell knew?

Crow had driven past Barrone's house first tonight. No lights on. No car in the driveway. Then Crow, restless again, had gone over to Stiles Island and done a drive-by at Billy Singer's rented house.

Also dark.

The Sonata Santo and Baldelli had been driving around town wasn't in the driveway. Maybe everybody was standing down now, just waiting until the vote, trying to run out the clock, making sure to stay out of Stone's way. And Crow's. Crow grinned at the mirror again. No *I* in *team*, he thought. But there were two in Wilson Cromartie. He'd have to remember to tell Stone that one.

He sat on Singer's street and called the bartender at the Scupper and asked if Santo and Baldelli had been in tonight. Bartender said no.

Crow turned the car around and went back over the bridge and headed for Lawton's house over there at Paradise Neck. The third stooge. Crow had started thinking of him and Billy and Barrone as the Three Stooges. Lawton was just the one Crow hadn't met. Stone said Crow wasn't missing anything.

Crow sat at the end of Lawton's drive for more than an hour. Nothing better to do. The lights were on in the house, upstairs and downstairs. Nobody in or out from the time Crow had showed up.

What am I?

Neighborhood watch?

He stayed for a few more minutes, knowing that all that was left after this was going back to the empty house and drinking from the flask and trying to get some sleep for a change.

Maybe I'm the one running out the clock, Crow thought.

65

Jesse was asleep when his cell phone blared at him from his bedside table at a little after two in the morning. It had taken him longer than usual to get to sleep tonight, thinking about how whoever was behind the killing had panicked, and the kids had panicked, and how it had maybe turned all of Paradise, Mass, into Stupidville.

He always turned up the ringer volume on the phone when he finally turned in, because he didn't want to miss some kind of emergency call.

Even though everything was starting to feel to him like a state of emergency, now he was running out of time before the vote, at which point everybody involved would likely scatter, at least in the short run.

The screen lit up when he grabbed the phone.

Unknown Caller

'This is Chief Stone,' he said.

'Wasn't calling to get your damn name, rank, and serial number,' he heard Tony Marcus say.

Jesse sat up now, rubbing his face hard, like he was trying to rub the grogginess away.

'I come across a couple things for you on my boy Darnell Woodson,' Tony said, 'might help you out.'

'He's pretty much still a ghost,' Jesse said.

He heard Marcus chuckle. 'Least you didn't call him no spook.'

Jesse waited.

'I talked to Sunny Randall herself about you,' Tony said.

Means he's had more contact with her than I have.

Marcus said, 'Girl told me if I could find it in my heart to do a favor for you, she might do another one for me one of these days.'

'I could owe you one,' Jesse said.

'Nah,' Tony said. 'You might say you would. But you wouldn't give it up in the end.'

'No way for you to know that,' Jesse said.

'She does, though,' Marcus said. 'Said you was the last Boy Scout.'

'I still came to you,' Jesse said.

'Anyway, here's what I come up with for you,' Marcus said. 'Turns out Darnell was down here the other night, one of the clubs I got a piece of, buying drinks for people, telling them he was about to cash out.'

Jesse waited.

'You with me?' Marcus said.

'I'm here.'

'He said his shit had finally come in,' Marcus said. 'Said he got himself one of those whales they talk about in Vegas.'

'Did he mention Billy Singer's name when he was talking about whales?' Jesse said. 'Or Ed Barrone's?'

'Think it was more like a figger of speech,' Tony Marcus said.

'What about Thomas Lawton?' Jesse said.

'I had a name, I would have given it up,' Tony Marcus said. 'Who the fuck knows? Maybe Darnell got with all of them. He always was a transactional sumbitch.'

'Thank you for this,' Jesse said.

First I'm in business with Crow. Now Tony Marcus. Maybe I'm not the last Boy Scout after all.

Marcus said, 'Darnell made it sound like he was taking early retirement for real this time, sooner rather than later.'

'You wouldn't happen to have an address for Woodson,' Jesse said.

'Boy's address is usually wherever he's shacked up and getting his damn ashes hauled,' Marcus said.

Jesse said, 'You said you had something else.'

'So I did,' Marcus said.

He waited again.

'Darnell also might have said he had some unfinished business with the cops up there,' Tony Marcus said, 'on account of what happened with his boy Richie.'

Then Tony Marcus said, 'Adios,' and was gone.

66

Thomas Lawton and Billy Singer and Ed Barrone were all in Jesse's office the next morning.

They weren't happy about being summoned. Lawton was threatening to call the mayor. Jesse didn't expect to accomplish much, or learn anything. He had just awakened with the urge to bounce them around a little bit. And look them all in the eyes again.

Lawton had told Jesse the same thing he'd told him after Molly shot Richie Carr, that he didn't know Carr, had never done business with Carr.

Jesse turned to Billy Singer and Barrone.

'I've already asked Mr Lawton this,' he said to them. 'But is there any chance I might discover that one of you boys has a connection to Carr or Darnell Woodson or both?'

'Billy's the one who brought hired thugs into this,' Barrone said. 'I didn't play it that way.'

'Didn't play it that way this time, you mean,' Singer said.

'Fuck off,' Barrone said.

'Moving right along,' Jesse said.

'Did the girl wake up yet?' Lawton said to Jesse.

'Not yet,' Jesse said. 'And maybe not ever.'

'You mind explaining why we're all here?' Barrone said.

'Is that an existential question?' Jesse said.

'Huh?' Barrone said.

'At least one of you sent somebody to Neil O'Hara's house

looking for something, and then to Ben Gage's,' Jesse said. 'Finally to Kate O'Hara's. I was just wondering why.'

'You got no proof of that,' Barrone said. 'You got no proof tying anybody in this room to what happened to the mayor and those kids. All's I can see here is you busting chops.'

Lawton said, 'Everybody's got to be good at something.'

Jesse smiled. 'What are you good at, Thomas?'

'Listen,' Lawton said, leaning forward in his chair. 'I had no use for that kid. For any of those kids, truth be told. But I liked Neil, whether you want to believe that or not, and even though he was on the wrong side of this.'

'He was just a small-town guy who couldn't think big enough,' Billy Singer said.

'You mean he wasn't like the big thinkers I've got sitting across from me,' Jesse said.

'Listen,' Singer said, 'because I'm going to say this for the last time. None of us in this room are saints.' He threw a derisive nod at Jesse. 'Excepting you, of course. And even though Barrone or me is going to end up a loser on this thing, nobody this close to closing a sweetheart deal like this is going to be enough of a dumbass to kill people before we do.'

'And on that note,' Lawton said, checking his phone, 'and if you're done wasting our time, I call this meeting adjourned.'

Jesse smiled again.

'One of you knows exactly what's going on here,' Jesse said. 'I just wonder why the other two aren't more worried about that. Or wonder what the threat might be to this deal getting locked down.'

Ed Barrone stood.

'Your problem, Chief,' he said, 'not ours. And by the way? Your Indian friend ever comes near me again, I'm not calling you to complain, I'm calling my friend the governor.'

'I'll give him a stern talking-to,' Jesse said.

Thomas Lawton stood. So did Singer.

'Thanks for wasting our time,' Singer said.

'A meeting about nothing,' Lawton said, 'because you've got nothing.'

'You sure about that?' Jesse said.

67

Because of what Tony Marcus had said about Darnell Woodson, whom Jesse believed was on his way back to Paradise if not here already, he had told Crow to keep an eye on Molly.

When Jesse told Molly about it, realizing what kind of plague she'd wish on Jesse if she found out on her own, there was hardly any pushback at her end of the line.

'He was talking about money and about revenge, Molls,' Jesse said. 'Not a good combination, from my experience.'

'Not anybody's experience,' she said.

'I can't do what I have to do, whatever the hell I'm doing right now,' Jesse said, 'and be worrying about you when you're not at the station.'

'Got it,' she said.

'So you're really not going to fight me on this?' he said.

'I already told you I wouldn't,' Molly said. 'Take the win.'

She said she was going to spend the rest of her day under the watchful eye of Crow, obsessing a little more about Blair Richmond.

'And you can go try to catch bad guys,' she said.

'I'd settle for catching a break at this point,' Jesse said.

She was calling him from home.

'Crow out front?' Jesse said.

'You know he is.'

'You could invite him in for breakfast,' Jesse said.

'You're aware you keep sending me mixed messages on that guy,' she said.

'Keeps the spark in the relationship.'

Molly said, 'Yours with me or yours with him?'

Jesse got a call then from Terry Harvey, asking if there'd been any new developments.

'I wish,' Jesse said. 'Some new information has come in, but none of it applies to you, at least not yet.'

'I'll pray that you get some help from the spirit world,' Harvey said.

'Send all the spirits you can,' Jesse said.

He heard the tribal leader laugh.

'When you say it like that, it sounds like what we used to call fire water,' Harvey said.

Gabe Weathers, Jesse knew, was into Richie Carr's Land Cruiser over at the impound lot in Marshport, had been there since seven in the morning. Gabe said he'd call if he came up with anything useful.

Jesse sat at his desk for a long time, studying his case notes on both Neil O'Hara and Ben Gage. Sketching out one more timeline that made sense to him. He knew exactly when Neil had died. It was less clear with Ben Gage. Jesse wondered if they'd died the same night. And if Ben Gage hadn't died that night, where had he gone? What made him run, and hide, at least until somebody found him? And if he had things to hide, where had he hidden them?

Had Blair met up with him before he was beaten and shot and buried over in Marshport?

Jesse felt the sudden need to move now, put himself in motion, maybe search the houses again, go bother Lawton, or Singer, or Barrone. Crow was watching Molly. He would bet everything in his wallet that they would take a ride over to the hospital to look in on Blair Richmond, because both of them had been over there every day.

What would she be able to tell them when she woke up, if she ever did?

He would start at Neil's house. He kept being drawn back

there, still thinking he'd missed something, that there might be a clue hiding in plain sight. That the walls might still talk to him. Or Neil's spirit might talk, now that Terry Harvey had talked about putting the spirit world into play.

When he pulled up now in front of the house on Beach Avenue, he saw that Gabe Weathers was waiting for him

'Got a question,' he said, 'and an observation.'

Jesse told him that if it was a hard question, Gabe was frankly wasting his time.

68

Gabe's observation to Jesse had been that Richie Carr's navigation system had turned into a dead end. There had *been* one in the SUV, but Carr – or someone – had removed it.

'So he was a punk,' Gabe said, 'but a punk smart enough of a tech guy not to leave a trail.'

'Not that it did him much good in the end,' Jesse said.

'I wish there had been a trail to a car wash once in a while,' Gabe said. 'Man was a pig.'

'That's the observation,' Jesse said. 'What's the question?'

'How come we never checked Neil's car?' Gabe said.

'Suit and Pete Perkins went over it, top to bottom, two or three times,' Jesse said.

'I meant the car's computer,' Gabe said.

'I was in that car with him,' Jesse said. 'It's a heap.'

'It's actually newer than it looks,' Gabe said. 'A '17 Chevy Volt.'

'Neil used to call it a Chevy Dolt,' Jesse said, 'and kept threatening to get a new one with more bells and whistles.'

'I looked it up,' Gabe said. 'This one happens to *have* bells and whistles.'

Jesse stared at him.

'We should have checked the car's computer,' Gabe said.

'But I didn't tell you to.'

'And nobody stopped me from bringing it up before this.'

'I just missed it,' Jesse said.

'Happens to the best of us.' Gabe grinned. 'Reason I know that is because you *are* the best of us.'

They went inside Neil O'Hara's garage. Jesse stood next to Neil's Chevy. Gabe got behind the wheel, Gabe having gotten his toolkit out of his own car, prepared to take apart as much of the dashboard as he could.

'We needed a subpoena for Carr's ride,' Gabe said. 'Not this one?'

'Not today we don't,' Jesse said.

'What if we find something we can use?'

Jesse said, 'Let's find something we can use first and worry about the rest of it with our friend the district attorney later.'

'You're the chief,' Gabe said.

'Aren't I, though,' Jesse said.

Gabe had his laptop next to him on the passenger seat. He was on the phone with an ex-cop he'd once partnered with in the old days, now working for a company in Boston that specialized in reconstructing car accidents. Gabe had him on speaker. Jesse was no idiot when it came to gadgets, but they had lost him about five minutes into their conversation about data transparency and special software and circuit boards and GM versus Ford, and even vehicle AI.

The guy's name was Jim Silliman.

At one point Jesse heard Silliman say, 'Unfortunately the computer for this baby is buried deep under the dash.'

Gabe told him he'd already figured that out on his own.

'So prepare yourself for a lot of prying and unscrewing that still may turn out to be a wild-goose chase,' Silliman said over the speaker. 'By the way? Is the guy whose car this is ever gonna want to use it again?'

'The guy died,' Jesse said.

'Who's that?' Jim said.

'My boss,' Gabe said.

'The old ballplayer you told me about?' Jim said.

'Just old,' Jesse said.

'This could be slightly illegal even if the person is deceased,' Jim said.

'We're all going to look the other way a little bit for the time being,' Jesse said.

'I can do that,' Silliman said.

'Jim,' Jesse said, 'if we get lucky, can this system maybe tell us where the car has been lately?'

'Maybe. Depends on what was activated and what wasn't.'

There was a pause.

Silliman said, 'No shit, I know you're the chief, Chief, but there really could be privacy statutes that come into play here.'

'Fuck 'em,' Jesse said.

'How come I never got to work for somebody like you?' Silliman said.

'It's truly a blessing,' Gabe said, winking at Jesse.

Gabe Weathers was as cool as anybody Jesse had. And as good a cop. Maybe a better cop than anybody he had. Long hair, beard, his latest bomber jacket, cowboy boots of his own. And a pitbull on any case he was working, or on any problem he was trying to solve.

'This could take a whole day,' Jim Silliman said over the speaker. 'Or more.'

Jesse said, 'We'll pay you for your time.'

'If it helps you catch whoever did it,' Jim said, 'it's on me. Once a cop, always a cop.'

Gabe went to work. He told Jesse there was no point in him hanging around.

'You're sure I can't help?' Jesse said, and Gabe said, 'Very sure.' Then he told Jesse he would work on this as long as his own bad back let him and call it a night and if he hadn't gotten anywhere, he would be back first thing in the morning, and for as long as it took.

'You know this could be another dead end,' Gabe said.

'Molly says that faith is believing what you can't see,' Jesse told him.

Gabe told him to beat it, he'd call if he got something, that for now it was just putting one of his favorite fundamentals of police work into play.

'Which one?' Jesse said.

Gabe said, 'Throwing shit against the wall and hoping some of it sticks.'

69

Crow and Molly were at the hospital. Jesse called Molly's phone, and asked if Blair had improved. No, Molly said, but she hasn't gotten any worse, either. The doctors said it was a good thing, at least for now.

'Now you take the win,' Jesse said to her.

He was sitting on his terrace by then, in the late afternoon, listening to the ocean. He still loved doing that, never got tired of doing it, probably never would get tired of it. He'd loved looking at the water and listening to it and walking the beaches when he'd lived in Los Angeles, too. It usually could fill him with a sense of calm.

Just not right now.

Right now he felt like he was underwater.

Maybe he was getting old.

Maybe this was the case he couldn't solve. Or wouldn't. Maybe this time he couldn't get justice for the victims, and somebody was going to get away with murder.

It had happened before. Jesse would probably die himself

thinking Bryce Cain, another spoiled rich boy from Paradise, had gotten away with killing his mother and his half-brother a couple years before.

But he was honest enough with himself, most of the time, anyway, to realize that it was about more than the pursuit of justice that drove him. He needed *to know*. He needed to figure things out. Put the puzzle together. Molly and Suit kept telling him that he'd almost always figured things out in the past. But those cases didn't matter to him now. Your lifetime batting average in baseball didn't help you in the season you were playing, when you were looking to get a hit. *This* case was the one that mattered. Neil mattered. Ben Gage mattered.

Blair Richmond mattered most of all, because she was still here.

And if that land did belong to the tribe, if it was just one more piece of property in America that had been stolen from them, well, that sure seemed as if it ought to matter, too.

Gut instinct told him that Dix was right. The killer, or killers, probably did shoot Neil in the head before they could put their hands on whatever Ben Gage had found. Get rid of him, get rid of both of them, worry about finding the proof later. If somebody else knew something, they would have come forward by now. All Terry Harvey knew was that Neil thought he had something big, and was prepared to show him.

Show and tell.

But if they'd found what they were looking for at Ben Gage's house, why had they gone after Kate?

Santo and Baldelli?

Or Richie Carr and Darnell Woodson?

And did Ed Barrone have his own thugs working this, even if he said he didn't, and they'd been good enough that Jesse hadn't seen them yet?

Jesse tried to remember the Irish word Molly had for this kind of mess, but couldn't.

He got up. He still needed to move, even if he knew he was probably just going to spin his wheels a little more. He got into the Explorer and drove back over to Ben and Blair's house, and used the key he had to open the door and go through it himself now the way he'd gone through Neil's, room by room, and then out into the small backyard. He stood in the middle of the yard and stared at the treehouse Blair had talked about, where they'd gone to dream their dreams.

He climbed the ladder, excited suddenly.

But there was nothing much to see with the exception of a heart carved into the wooden floor, with 'Ben' and 'Blair' inside, and a date, and this written underneath:

Forever.

He locked up the house and got back into the Explorer, thinking about an Apache expression Crow had given him the other day, about how in this world it is the unseen that have the power.

Do they ever, Jesse thought.

He was halfway back to the station, because he couldn't think of anywhere else to go right now, when Crow called from the hospital.

'She's awake,' he said.

70

Day of the vote.

Mayor Gary Armistead had decided to make the event public, even allowing it to be streamed live from Paradise.gov.

Townspeople who wanted one last chance to weigh in on the merits of the sale, or lack thereof, had been invited to show up and address all of them on the stage: Armistead, the other members of the Board, Lawton, Singer, Barrone, all of whom would be up onstage. They had pulled down the bleachers in the gym at Paradise High, and set up folding chairs that stretched from the stage all the way back to the double doors that opened up into the lobby.

Jesse watched from the back of the gym.

The first order of business had been Billy Singer and Ed Barrone addressing the Board and the townspeople gathered in front of them for the last time, explaining why each man thought he was the best person to develop the land. Why their plan was best for the town. They were both cheered when introduced, with only a smattering of boos.

Singer had gone first. Barrone had finished his brief talk by saying, 'I'm from around here. You people know me.'

'Which is why they should be rooting for me,' Singer said into his handheld microphone.

It actually got a laugh.

Now it was the citizens of Paradise being heard, the line of people waiting to speak stretching down the middle aisle. Men and women. Old people and young. Old money and older. Rich and un-rich.

Stepping to the microphone now was Daisy Dyke. She was wearing denim painter's pants with lots of pockets and an SOB T-shirt. Her hair was streaked with magenta today. When she'd taken her place in the line, she'd turned and winked at Jesse, who'd snapped off a salute in response. She'd then grinned and given him the finger.

'There are things that make this town special, leastways I think they do,' she said. 'And the things that make it most special are the ones that shouldn't be for sale. Now I've been listening to both sides of this for months, and here's what I've finally decided. The real SOBs in this thing are sitting over there to the side of the stage.'

She pointed at Lawton, Singer, Barrone.

'I listened to Mr Singer and Mr Barrone a few minutes ago and, for the life of me, still can't figure out who the hell they're talking to,' Daisy said. 'Because they are sure not talking to *me*.'

A lot of the people in the gym cheered. Daisy walked up near the stage, eyeballed Lawton and Singer and Barrone one last time, then walked back to where Jesse was standing.

'You should be mayor,' he said to her.

'No shit, Sherlock,' she said.

There were a couple more speakers. When they finished Gary Armistead said, 'Now it's time to get down to business. First, I and the other members of the Paradise Board of Selectmen will cast our votes, by a show of hands, on whether to approve the sale of the land in question by Thomas Lawton.'

Then he held up two envelopes for everybody in the gym to see.

'When *that* piece of business is concluded,' he said, 'I will open these sealed envelopes, which I promise have not been opened since Mr Singer and Mr Barrone submitted them last week, and we will all find out, in real time, who has made the winning bid for Mr Lawton's land.'

Armistead smiled directly at the camera to his left.

'Shall we get this party started?' he said.

It was then that the double doors next to Jesse opened and Terry Harvey, carrying a large cardboard box, came walking in, followed by Rita Fiore of Cone, Oakes in all of her sassy, spectacular, red-haired glory. Jesse knew that the older man with them, someone who looked as if he could have been Crow's father, or at least an older brother, was Jason Ahanu Thompson, a Tribal Historic Preservation Officer.

'I'm ready for my close-up,' she said to Jesse before she and Terry Harvey and Jason Ahanu Thompson walked up the center aisle toward the stage.

71

Jesse had called Rita after Harvey had informed him about his brief career at Cone, Oakes, telling her that she needed to be at the ready if he could prove that The Throw might very well be the property of the Peccontac Nation.

'No one,' Rita said, 'is more at the ready for you than I.'

'I meant going into legal battle,' Jesse said.

'Well, I didn't,' she said.

She stepped to the microphone now as if she were the one being given an award, maybe as the most impressive woman on the North Shore.

'My name is Rita Fiore, kids,' she said. 'As a way of introduction, I am a senior partner at the Boston law firm of Cone, Oakes, which, for those of you not familiar with our work, is about as formidable as a SWAT team.'

She nodded to her left, then to her right. She was wearing a short black dress and high heels. Her hair was even longer than he remembered. Her long legs were, as Jesse remembered, quite formidable themselves.

'Standing next to me,' she continued, 'is Mr Terry Harvey of the Peccontac Tribal Nation, which once settled the land being discussed today. Mr Thompson here is a Tribal Historic Preservation Officer. And the three of us are here to tell everybody in this gym and everybody who might be watching that no one is selling that land today, or buying it, because I was in court a little over an hour ago to get a temporary restraining order. And the reason I *was* able to get one is because Mr Harvey is now in possession of certain precious tribal objects and remains that Mr Thompson says prove that the land in question has really always belonged to the Peccontac people and not the original robber baron in Mr Lawton's family.'

'You have no right!' Mayor Gary Armistead yelled.

Even from this far away, Jesse thought Lawton's face had quickly turned the color of Rita's hair. Jesse couldn't understand what Singer and Barrone were saying, because they kept shouting over each other.

'And who are you, Sparky?' Rita said to Gary Armistead.

'I'm the mayor of this town!' Gary Armistead said.

'Good for you,' Rita said. 'So you should know, Mr Mayor, that the judge's exact words were that if anybody even thought about touching that land before he rules on a permanent injunction next week, that they might be sitting in a county jail until the Fourth of July.'

Jesse was staring at Lawton and Singer and Barrone, whom he thought might have calcified now that they'd sat back down. Rita had their full attention now. She had everybody's attention. Generally she got it just by walking into a room.

Terry Harvey reached into the box and handed her a piece of paper, which Rita held up for the crowd to see.

'There are copies of the TRO in the lobby,' she said. 'I underlined the place where Judge Thompson said that based on the evidence we submitted to him this morning, the possibility of the plaintiff – Mr Harvey, in this case – succeeding on the merits of his case are overwhelming.'

'It's not his land!' Thomas Lawton said from the stage, standing and rousing himself all over again. 'It's *mine*, goddamn it!'

'Not,' Rita said.

Jesse watched now as a side door up near the stage opened and Crow came walking out carrying a long folding table that he set up in front of Rita and Terry Harvey and Jason Ahanu Thompson, between them and the stage.

Then Crow helped Harvey take things out of the box and lay them gently on top of the table, items that Ben Gage had unearthed at The Throw across the last week of his life.

'*What is that junk?*' Ed Barrone roared.

'Manners,' Rita said, as she turned the standup microphone back to Terry Harvey.

'The ones wrapped in leather are human remains that we will prove come from the Peccontac tribe,' Terry Harvey said, almost reverently. 'There is also wampum jewelry. A copper arm cuff. Beaded jewelry. A couple of pottery items, as you can plainly see, with grains inside. Thanks to Ms. Fiore, more items are currently being unearthed from what was clearly a burial site for our people.'

Jesse hadn't noticed Gary Armistead's gavel before. He was banging it now. And yelling for order, though as far as Jesse could tell, the only one out of order in the moment was him.

People had already begun to file up and inspect the items, Crow standing at a corner of the table with his arms crossed. Jesse had made his way up past the bleachers, and was now standing at the foot of the stage, below Thomas Lawton and Billy Singer and Ed Barrone. He noticed the two envelopes in front of Gary Armistead next to his own microphone, still unopened.

'You did this,' Lawton said when he noticed Jesse standing there.

'No,' Jesse said. 'The tree huggers did.'

Then he pointed an imaginary gun at him and Singer and Barrone with his fingers.

'Bang,' Jesse said. 'Now *you're* all dead.'

72

Blair Richmond had spoken slowly when she was awake, some of the words difficult to understand because of some paralysis on the right side of her face that Dr Abramson said he hoped would go away eventually.

At one point she looked up at Crow and said, 'You're that Indian man.'

'Yes,' he said.

'I thought you were bad,' she said.

Jesse saw Crow smile.

'But in a good way,' he said.

She knew by now, from Dr Abramson and the nurses, what had happened to her. They had told her that Molly had likely saved her life. Blair had thanked Molly.

'Our job is to preserve and protect,' Molly said. 'I only did the first part.'

'Chief Stone,' Blair said now.

'I'm here,' Jesse said.

Then she had told them as much as she could remember, stopping every few sentences because even that seemed to exhaust her, or couldn't find the right word. Jesse told her she didn't have to do this right now. She said she wanted to at least try.

She jumped around. She kept stopping. She would get confused. Almost disoriented. Her timeline was off. She would back up and start over again. She kept saying she knew she was forgetting things. She told them she had planned to walk to her house after she left Jesse's office that day when she got back from Providence. Sam and Diane Burrows were going to pick her up there.

But she had gotten a call from Ben, telling her *not* to go back to the house, it wasn't safe for either one of them, that they'd come for Mr O'Hara and then come for him. He told her to find a way to meet him at their cabin.

'It was the one he and his dad had built over in Oxbow,' Blair said. 'Where you found me. He always called it our safe house.' She squeezed her eyes shut. 'Until it wasn't.'

They thought for a moment she'd gone back to sleep.

'I should have called you sooner,' Blair said to Molly.

'You did just fine,' Molly said.

'I don't know how the man found me,' Blair said.

She was talking to herself now.

'Richie Carr,' Molly said quietly.

Blair once again looked confused.

'He's the man who shot you,' Molly said. 'Before I shot him.'

Blair said, 'He wanted to know where Ben had hidden it. I told him I didn't know what "it" was. He said he'd shoot me if I didn't tell. I screamed at him that I didn't know, no matter how many times he asked me.'

She was starting to slur her words more as she went.

'Is he the one who killed Ben?' she said.

'Him or his partner,' Jesse said.

Blair said, 'I shouldn't have been so much like Ben. With the police. I should have called sooner for help.'

'Live and learn,' Jesse said. 'Heavy on the living part.'

The nurse came in then, and told them Blair needed sleep. Blair thanked her again for saving her life. They all told her they'd come see her again tomorrow.

'But I'm not finished,' she said.

Then she told them about the wishing tree.

73

As they were leaving, Blair had said she needed to start her story all over again, that she remembered parts that she'd left out. Jesse told her she could do it tomorrow. Or when she was fully up to it. She said she wanted to do it right now.

'In case I forget stuff for good,' she said.

Then she told them that the last time Ben had called her he sounded more frantic than ever, but made sure to tell her that he'd left one last note for her in their wishing tree that would explain everything about what he called buried treasure if something happened to him. She told him to stop talking like that. Yelled at him that this wasn't some game, it had stopped being a game a long time ago, *what* treasure?

She squeezed her eyes shut.

'But I was talking to myself by then,' she said. 'He was gone.'

When she found out he was dead, she'd hidden in the cabin until she called Molly Crane. Blair kept repeating that she should have called Molly sooner. Molly kept telling her that fear could make even brave people go a little bit crazy.

Jesse had gone over to the house after leaving the hospital, had found the tree with the small slot carved into it, the envelope with the key inside, and a locker number from Safe Storage, located in the Swap. It was there that Ben Gage had stored the artifacts he'd dug up.

'He had to have shown Neil some of what he had,' Jesse aid.

'But not told him where he had it stashed?' Crow said.

'Maybe the only person he trusted completely was Blair,' Jesse said.

They both knew how much they would never know about the last night of Neil O'Hara's life, the last days of Ben Gage's. Jesse was going on the assumption, what he thought was a reasonable one, that Ben must have hidden at least one key after discovering that his house had been searched. And run. Until Carr and Woodson had caught up with him. Tying up one more loose end.

'It can only be them,' Jesse said to Crow.

'Turns out that maybe Santo and Baldelli caught a good beating from me for nothing,' Crow said.

'Might make them work harder at being their best selves,' Jesse said.

Billy Singer was back in Vegas by now. Ed Barrone had announced he was putting his casino in Taunton up for sale. Thomas Lawton's lawyers were trying to get the restraining order thrown out, as a way of somehow bringing the deal back to life, but were being outlawyered by Rita Fiore at every turn, as Jesse knew they would be.

'All those big winners,' Crow said now, 'coming up losers in the end. Like they were all in Vegas.'

He had come over tonight to say goodbye, telling Jesse he was leaving in the morning.

'You gonna say goodbye to Molly?' Jesse said.

'Already did.'

'How'd that go?' Jesse said.

'She thanked me for everything I did saving your life and told me she was glad the two of us were on better terms and then told me to never come back,' Crow said.

'Kind of gets you right here,' Jesse said.

He was drinking one of those cold-brew coffees he'd taken a liking to. Crow kept sipping on his flask. Sometimes they would go for a few minutes without either one of them speaking. It made neither one of them jumpy.

Finally Crow said, 'Somebody still got away with murder.'

'Two murders,' Jesse said. 'And nearly a third.'

'Somebody hired Carr and Woodson,' Crow said. 'Bother you, you don't know who did that, either?'

Jesse gave him a sideways look. 'What do you think?'

Gabe had called that morning to tell him he was throwing in the towel on Neil O'Hara's car, as pissed off as he was to be telling Jesse that. But he and Jim Silliman had come up empty, goddamn it all to hell.

'At least none of those bastards got away with murder on the land deal,' Jesse said. 'So we've got that going for us.'

'Because of a note the kid left in a tree,' Crow said.

'One tree hugger leaving it for another,' Jesse said.

'The kid digging those graves finally dug up something that buried them all,' Crow said.

'Pity,' Jesse said. 'Isn't it?'

'Ben Gage turned out to be a hero in this,' Crow said.

'So did Neil,' Jesse said.

'So did the girl,' Crow said.

'Where you headed next?' Jesse said.

He saw Crow smile.

'Thought I might head down to the Florida Keys and buy myself a little fishing boat,' Crow said. 'Try some of that Hemingway shit on for size.'

'Old injun and the sea,' Jesse said.

'Old Kiowa,' Crow said.

'Or Jicarilla.'

Crow stood up. He put out his hand. Jesse shook it.

'Next time,' Crow said.

Jesse smiled again.

'Do we really need one?' Jesse said.

Jesse was still on his terrace, Crow long gone, when he heard the banging on his door. Gabe Weathers was standing there when he opened it, along with a big, bald guy he introduced as Jim Silliman. They were both grinning at him. Gabe had some printouts in his hand.

'Quitters never win,' Gabe said.

74

Jesse left the Explorer on the road and walked up from there, not wanting to announce that he was here. He noticed a single light on in the gatehouse tonight, but no car parked in its driveway. The big house was fully lit, though.

When Thomas Lawton opened the door, Jesse could see suitcases in the front hall.

'Get lost,' Lawton said to Jesse. 'I've got nothing to say to you. Like ever again.'

'Maybe you do,' Jesse said.

'Who's there, Tommy?' Jesse heard.

Kate O'Hara had come walking out of the living room with a glass of wine in her hand.

She stopped when she saw Jesse. Opened her mouth and closed it.

'You two kids going somewhere?' Jesse said. 'Have you really thought this through, Kate? He's not as rich as you thought he was going to be.'

'Whatever,' Lawton said. 'The one who's going right now is you.'

Lawton started to shut the door.

Jesse put an arm out and stopped him.

'Tommy?' he said. 'You don't want to upset me tonight.'

He walked past him and into the living room and left them little choice but to follow him.

'You told me Neil's world was getting smaller,' Jesse said to Kate.

'What you do want, Jesse?' she said.

'Thinking closure,' Jesse said.

Lawton reached for the phone on the coffee table, started to punch out some numbers.

'I'm calling the mayor,' he said.

Jesse smiled.

'Tommy,' he said, 'if you don't put down that phone I will make you eat it.'

'What's this about, Stone?' he said. 'You want to rub my face in it one last time? Unless I drop the case against the goddamn Indians, I'll be in federal court for the rest of my life. And that's the best-case scenario. I lost. You won. Game over.'

'Not quite yet,' Jesse said.

Then he took the printouts Gabe and Jim Silliman had brought with them out of the side pocket of his windbreaker, the ones they'd handed over to Jesse after they'd finally cracked the code on Neil O'Hara's navigation system and been able to determine the last several stops the car had made.

The last few stops, time-stamped, were the only ones that had interested Jesse.

The final one had been at Neil's house on Beach Avenue. The one before that had been at The Throw, which meant the killer or killers had driven him there in his own car.

The one before that had been at the home he had once shared with Kate O'Hara on Stiles Island, still listed as 'Home,' as it turned out, in the car's computer because Neil had never changed it. Or maybe remained hopeful that it could be his home again someday, provided she took him back.

He unfolded the printouts and spread them out on the coffee table, explaining what they were. Lawton looked down at them. Kate O'Hara kept staring at Jesse.

Out of his other pocket, Jesse pulled out the black-and-white photographs that he'd gotten from the guard gate at The Bluffs from the night when Neil O'Hara had been shot to death. One showed Neil behind the wheel of the Chevy Volt at 8:35. A half-hour later there were Richie Carr behind the wheel of Carr's Highlander, the man Jesse now knew to be Darnell Woodson in the passenger seat next to him.

Kate O'Hara, as beautiful as ever, was still staring at him.

'I wasn't there,' she said. 'I had driven over here to see Thomas after your friend Crow stopped by earlier.'

Jesse knew what he had and what he didn't have. He was just here hoping one of them would make a mistake. She'd lied to him before.

'No,' he said. 'I checked. Your car never came back through the gate that night. Neither did your boyfriend's. You didn't leave and you were still there when I came to tell you about Neil.'

'Please stop talking, Kate,' Lawton said.

Jesse ignored him.

'I screwed up here,' he said. 'I realize that now. You always look at the husband or wife first. But this was different. I knew you. So I never thought he could have gone to see you that night.

214

You know what I'm guessing? Neil had good news to share with you that night. Ben Gage had come around earlier to show him at least some of what he'd dug up. As soon as someone from the Peccontac Nation verified what the kid had, the deal was going to be dead in the water. Neil and the kids from SOB were going to stop the sale after all. And who better to share news like that with than his wife?'

'He wanted to have dinner,' Kate said. 'I told you that. I turned him down.'

'You know what else I think?' Jesse said, ignoring her. 'I think he told you some of it on the phone and told you he'd tell you the rest of it in person, and headed over to Stiles Island. But before he got there, you called Tommy, and told him Neil was about to go public with some very bad shit that would mean that Tommy wasn't going to get his money after all.'

He smiled.

'You staged the break-in at your house, didn't you?' he said. 'What was the plan, to make yourself look like a victim? Or just get me to look anywhere except at you?'

She was the one looking away now.

'Okay,' Lawton said, 'we're done here. If you had more than this fairy tale, you would have arrested us already.'

Jesse said, 'Eventually. We went back over Neil's car, after we checked out the navigation. And guess what we came up with? DNA belonging to Mr Woodson that we'd missed.'

Jesse paused.

Fake it till you make it.

'And when I arrest Darnell,' Jesse continued, 'which I promise you I will, do either one of you really think he's going down for this alone?'

'Darnell's not going down for shit,' Darnell Woodson said, walking into the room, gun pointed at Jesse.

'You know the drill, Chief,' Woodson said. 'Hands where I can see 'em,' and then told Thomas Lawton to relieve the chief of his weapon and bring it over to him. Lawton did.

'I saw his car down to the road when I come in to pack up my shit,' Woodson said to Lawton. 'I figured nothing good could be happening up here.'

To Jesse, Woodson said, 'Man paid up what he owed me, though, even with his finances taking a turn for the worse like they did.' He shrugged. 'Least that deal went through.'

'You going to put a cop killing on top of everything else, Darnell?' Jesse said.

'Been reviewing my options fast as I can, Chief, and I got to admit, none of them good,' Woodson said.

He shook his head. Talking to himself.

'I don't know what my man Chief Stone has got for sure and what he don't got,' Darnell said, 'but either way, I don't see as how I can take no chances.'

He shook his head.

'Goddamn,' he said, 'this was all too good to be true. Even after Richie got hisself shot. Just too goddamn good to be true.'

Talking to himself more than the room.

'See,' Woodson said to Lawton and Kate, 'what neither of you know, or maybe just think you know, is that this man here will get up on everybody's shit and never get out. Whether he's got DNA or he don't, whether it's all circumstantial or not, he ain't quit now. And I don't want to spend the rest of my life looking over my *fucking* shoulder.'

'You got your cuffs with you?' he said to Jesse. Then he smiled. ''Course you do, probably never go anywhere without them. Thomas, go get 'em off the man's belt and cuff him behind his back, if that's just the same with you. I'm sorry it all come to this, but Chief Stone and me got to take a ride.'

Jesse stepped away from the fireplace as Lawton came around behind him. As he did, Jesse grabbed him, putting Lawton between him and Darnell Woodson, and rushed Lawton across the room, like a linebacker pushing a runner back even after the play was over. Woodson fired anyway, Kate screaming now, as Jesse felt the first bullet go through Thomas Lawton and hit

216

Jesse in his left shoulder, Jesse getting lower before the next bullet snapped Lawton's head back.

Lawton fell away. Jesse dropped and rolled to his side. Woodson kept firing. Jesse heard another scream from Kate then, saw her fall forward onto the coffee table, scattering the printouts and photographs, before there was one last gunshot from the front hall and Jesse saw that Woodson was down and Crow was standing over him.

75

They were in her big bed. Still in the big bed. Middle of Saturday afternoon. Had been in it pretty much nonstop since Friday night.

'Why did Darnell shoot her, too?' she said.

'At that point he seemed quite willing to shoot everybody, and with my gun,' Jesse said. 'The only people who could tie him to Neil and Ben Gage were in that room.'

'You think you actually could have proved any of it before the shooting started?' she said.

'Some,' Jesse said. 'Not all. And probably not nearly enough. But then Darnell walked in and the balloon went up.'

'Lawton wanted his money,' she said. 'Kate wanted him.' She smiled. 'Ain't love grand?'

'They both ended up dying over dirt,' Jesse said. 'Even if it did turn out to be sacred dirt.'

'The young woman is going to be all right?' she said.

'Gonna be a long rehab,' Jesse said. 'She's still got some paralysis in her face, and with her right arm and leg. Not sure if she makes it all the way back, frankly. But she's lucky to be alive. The doctors are amazed she's made it as far back as she already has.'

She gently touched his stitches. 'How's the war wound?' she said.

'Molly's was worse,' he said.

'Where's Crow?'

'Probably trying to hook a marlin,' Jesse said.

'It seems to bother you less and less with the passage of time that Crow was a killer once,' she said.

'Look who's talking, killer,' Jesse said.

'Weird sort of karma that Crow's Native American, don't you think?'

Jesse grinned. 'Karma or destiny,' he said.

'You think destiny brought us back together?' she said.

'Why not?' Jesse said.

Then he leaned over and got his face close to hers and said, 'Were you surprised to see me when I showed up?'

'Quite pleasantly surprised,' Rita Fiore said.

Then she said, 'Did you really break up with your girlfriend?'

Jesse grinned. 'It always ends up sounding like high school, doesn't it?'

'*Did* you break it off with her?'

'We're not even going to the prom,' Jesse said.

'I've got a dress that might fit the occasion.'

'I'll bet you do.'

'Want to see it?'

'Later.'

Rita's new town house was on Joy Street, on Beacon Hill, not terribly far from where Sunny lived. Rita said she'd chosen the house as much for the name of the street as for its location.

'What do you think the tribe will do with the land?' she said.

'They're unearthing stuff on a daily basis,' Jesse said. 'So they're reviewing their options.' He pulled her closer. 'As am I, as it turns out.'

'About time,' Rita said in a husky voice from somewhere underneath all that amazing red hair, and her whole amazing self.

'For what?' Jesse said.

'For me to put a little joy in your life, big boy,' she said.

And she did.

Acknowledgments

Once again, thanks to David and Daniel Parker, for trusting me with the high honor of writing about both Jesse Stone and Sunny Randall.

And to my agent, the great Esther Newberg, the gatekeeper for all of Robert B. Parker's characters.

These books could never be written without the wisdom and expertise and support of Capt. John Fisher, the Chief of Police in Carlisle, Mass.

And a special thanks this time to my friend Beau Doherty, who is steeped in Native American history, and Lori Potter, Public Affairs Director for the Mashantucket Pequot Tribal Nation.

Thanks to Tom Harvey, a lawyer who gets everybody's attention when he walks into court the way Rita Fiore does.

And finally my pals Peter Gethers, Scott Frank, David Koepp: Spitballers supreme.

NO EXIT PRESS

More than just the usual suspects

'A very smart, independent publisher delivering the finest literary crime fiction' – *Big Issue*

MEET NO EXIT PRESS, the independent publisher bringing you the best in crime and noir fiction. From classic detective novels to page-turning spy thrillers and singular writing that just grabs the attention. Our books are carefully crafted by some of the world's finest writers and delivered to you by a small, but mighty, team.

In over 30 years of business, we have published award-winning fiction and non-fiction including the work of a Pulitzer Prize winner, the British Crime Book of the Year, numerous CWA Dagger Awards, a British million copy bestselling author, the winner of the Canadian Governor General's Award for Fiction and the Scotiabank Giller Prize, to name but a few. We are the home of many crime and noir legends from the USA whose work includes iconic film adaptations and TV sensations. We pride ourselves in uncovering the most exciting new or undiscovered talents. New and not so new – you know who you are!!

We are a proactive team committed to delivering the very best, both for our authors and our readers.

Want to join the conversation and find out more about what we do?

Catch us on social media or sign up to our newsletter for all the latest news from No Exit Press HQ.

f fb.me/noexitpress **𝕏** @noexitpress
noexit.co.uk/newsletter

BECOME A
NO EXIT PRESS
MEMBER

BECOME A NO EXIT PRESS MEMBER and you will be joining a club of like-minded literary crime fiction lovers – and supporting an independent publisher and their authors!

AS A MEMBER YOU WILL RECEIVE

- Six books of your choice from No Exit's future publications at a discount off the retail price
- Free UK carriage
- A free eBook copy of each title
- Early pre-publication dispatch of the new books
- First access to No Exit Press Limited Editions
- Exclusive special offers only for our members
- A discount code that can be used on all backlist titles
- The choice of a free book when you first sign up

Gift Membership available too – the perfect present!

FOR MORE INFORMATION AND TO SIGN UP VISIT
noexit.co.uk/members